ALSO BY WILLIAM F. WELD

Mackerel by Moonlight

Big Ugly

Stillwater

A NOVEL

WILLIAM F. WELD

SIMON & SCHUSTER

NEW YORK LONDON TORONTO SYDNEY SINGAPORE

SIMON & SCHUSTER

Rockefeller Center

1230 Avenue of the Americas

New York, NY 10020

For information about special discounts for bulk purchases,

please contact Simon & Schuster Special Sales:

1-800-456-6798 or business@simonandschuster.com.

Designed by Karolina Harris

Manufactured in the United States of America

10   9   8   7   6   5   4   3   2   1

Library of Congress Cataloging-in-Publication Data

Weld, William F.

Stillwater: a novel / William F. Weld.

p. cm.

1. Teenage boys—Fiction. 2. Grandmothers—Fiction. 3. Massachusetts—

Fiction. 4. Reservoirs—Design and construction—Fiction. I. Title.

PS3573.E4547 S75 2002

813'.54—dc21   2001049275

ISBN 0-7432-0598-7

To Mary

Contents

Stillwater

The Swift River Valley

W H E N I was fifteen years old, I fell in love for the first and hardest time, I had my first tastes of inhumanity, and I watched every person I knew lose everything.

In a brief time I had the good fortune to see it all: the life that was lived in the five towns when we thought it would go on forever, the rumor of the plan to flood the Valley, the foreboding that grew like a fog around us, the destruction and flooding, and the aftermath. I could have lived ten lives and I would not have learned so much about endings and beginnings. The only other soul in the Valley who seemed to see it all was Hannah Corkery; she had had her share of endings and beginnings well before that summer.

They say in country towns, a man who dies today is buried

---

in the earth where he's lain many times before; the man who marries today takes the same wife he's taken for generations. Perhaps that made the powerful folks in Boston feel it didn't matter if they buried our homes.

One thing I've learned: you don't get to live a life that's all your own. There are hands pulling you back, hands pushing you forward. If you don't pick up your feet and walk, you'll be carried along, with no say as to where you're going.

———

Y o u would think nothing could prepare a child for what happened to us in 1938: the razing of our houses and farms, then the hurricane, then the flood. But I had had a sense for some time that events could go wrong. That was the way things were.

My mother ran off with a man to Pennsylvania when I was three, and I remembered not believing the explanations. I remembered watching from the window not long after as they brought my father in from the fields in a wheelbarrow. He had been killed in a threshing accident. They had folded him, so all I could see was his overalls. I recognized them well enough. I suppose it's as well I couldn't see more. I had woken up early from my afternoon nap and gone to the window in hopes of catching sight of some activity. Any sign of life would have been a diversion. Grandma saw me at the window and ran in the house and up to my room, engulfed me into her sobbing. She had on a gray calico housedress with pink flowers that I admired. I took in her scent. I thought it went with the dress. I accepted the fact I would not

be allowed to go downstairs or outside. That was how things
were. You lived life a moment at a time, at least in the Valley.
Then one day there was a death and it ended, at least as far
as you were concerned.

As the time for the flooding grew nearer, sometimes I
dreamed my father was coming to take me away, to help me
escape the water. I hadn't seen him in a dozen years. The fact
that he was dead made it neither more nor less likely, to my
mind, that he would return for me.

I never dreamed of my mother. It may be that I blamed her.
It's odd how the father seldom gets blamed, though in my
case his sin—being careless with the threshing machinery—
was great.

Grandma's reminiscing at the dinner table gave me a sense
of endings. She had enjoyed her days at the hat factory in
Dana. The girls who worked there were given a free palm leaf
hat for summer every year. That was as important to them as
the rest of their annual wage. In her new hat she had not
minded the trek along the main street to North Dana, to stop
by the soda fountain and say hello to the boys who could
occasionally afford to buy her a "white cow," vanilla iced
cream and ginger ale.

The hat shops were all gone by the late 1920s. People
wouldn't settle in the Valley once the Boston boys started
talking about putting us underwater. Grandma found work at
the Gee and Grover wooden box factory but said it wasn't the
same. I supposed it was the same, but you like best the thing
you do when you're young.

I could never work in a box factory. I don't understand
why people put so much effort into creating objects and arti-

facts from scratch, in imitation of the world we've been given free. The finest cloth ever spun is burlap compared to a beaver's pelt. The most skillful machine work imaginable cannot rival nature's turn of the lathe. You can reorganize nature's raw materials, as I did with my birch bark canoe, but you cannot create them.

Grandma said every man and woman she knew would consider themselves first and foremost a citizen of the Swift River Valley, second a resident of Hampshire County, or Franklin, or Hampden, or Worcester. The rest of the state, and for that matter the rest of the country and the world, could take care of themselves. Presumably would. The people of the Valley knew one another, knew the seasons and crops and animals, knew nature's rhythms, and so knew what was right. I did not need to have it spelled out for me that the "Boston boys" understood none of these things, particularly not the last.

Grandma had been married to Bill Hardiman, by all accounts a voluble and generous man, who had died of tuberculosis at the age of forty. His brother, Ed, was nothing like him: begrudging, if anything. But Grandma often invited Ed over to the farm for meals, as he lived alone.

Grandma was quiet during Uncle Ed's speeches on the lost virtues of country living. If it was after dinner she might pick up the pace on her knitting a notch or two. She was a polite soul, not wanting to point out that Uncle Ed had spent his working life as a municipal official, sitting at a desk all day. He had been the town clerk of Enfield for thirty years.

One evening we were talking at table about the news that the Valley might be flooded. "The history of the Swift River

Valley," Uncle Ed said, "is the history of man in God's world."

"The history of man in the natural world," said Grandma.

"The history of the Swift River Valley is the history of America," said Uncle Ed.

I hate to say it, but what Uncle Ed eventually did to the five Valley towns more or less proved that was true. America is grand and full, but people can be hard.

———

I grew up in the town of Enfield. Most of my friends lived across the line in Prescott or Ripton. We played Daniel Shays and General Benjamin Lincoln the way other boys played cowboys and Indians. Captain Shays, a decorated officer of the American Revolution, led the farmers' insurgency against the new government of the United States in 1787. He was a native of neighboring Pelham and our hero. General Lincoln, who had received Cornwallis's sword at Yorktown and handed it to General George Washington, may have been a hero in Boston. But he had hunted Shays down and so was evil incarnate in our play world. From the age of six or seven, Caleb Durand and I would dibs to play the part of Lincoln. That would give us license to practice a sneer.

Our towns had need of Captain Shays a century and a half later. That was when the government of Massachusetts announced a plan to send more men west from Boston, this time to flood the Valley to create a reservoir sixteen miles long, better to assuage the thirst of the patriotic citizens of Boston.

Caleb and Hannah and I understood what was being done

———

to our families better than most of the grown-ups in the Valley. We had the history in our bones, having acted it out many times in the woods. We knew that having your hometown flooded is worse than having your family die, because there's nothing to visit, not even a gravestone.

I said to Hannah that attachment to the land is the same as attachment to one's ancestors, if you have family roots in a place. She held that they were different, because you have no choice but to be connected to your ancestors and your descendants, whereas you can always pick up and move. Not if you're attached to the land because of your ancestors, I said. And so the argument moved in a circle.

I learned a lot in 1938 about the surface of the earth: its folds and tissues, its dips and catchments. Of course, the water covered all that, covered Dana, Enfield, Greenwich, Ripton, and most of Prescott. Before they closed the locks at Winsor Dam, though, I could have led you to every cave, tunnel, quarry, and mine shaft in the Valley. Partly that was my own enterprise, mine and Caleb's; partly it was our good fortune in joining forces with Hammy, who was as comfortable below ground as above it.

When I was playing in the leaves or the mud as a child, sometimes I would pretend the earth was about to open and swallow me up. That would make me tingle. Hannah said that was the spirits' way of telling me what was going to happen. It turned out she was right, as usual.

When Captain Shays walked the earth, all the land in the Valley had been put to the plow. Everything was farms, seldom separated by more than a tumbledown stone wall or a hedgerow. In the time since Shays, the woods had flooded back onto the land, carrying along their cargo of wolves, coyotes, and catamount. You could chart nature's counterattack by the number of cellar holes in the woods: every one of them had marked the heart of a working farm.

As surely as ancient soldiers sowed salt in vanquished fields, nature leaves nothing to chance as it recaptures its territory. In cellars and foundations below the ground, vines and creepers were constantly at work to separate and dislodge the man-ordered stones. You can subjugate a piece of property easily enough, but if you don't tend it, nature's gods will wrest it from you in a twinkling.

———

I suppose I must have learned a bit at the Enfield school, since I went into teaching. You couldn't prove it by me at the time, though. I thought the lessons at school emphasized what was unimportant or dull. Or plainly untrue, like what they taught us in civics class.

Grandma encouraged me to read every day from the end of school until the beginning of evening chores. She had read me Kenneth Grahame's *Wind in the Willows* years earlier, and bribed me to learn by heart long passages from its seventh chapter, "The Piper at the Gates of Dawn." I took different lessons from this book every time I opened it. I was encouraged also to return to Conan Doyle's *King Arthur,* Ernest Thompson Seton's *Wild Animals I Have Known,* and to wander about in Frazer's *Golden Bough.* These reinforced my excitement with the natural world.

My other source of books was Annie Richards, the sheriff's

———

wife, who lent me *Gone with the Wind, The Virginian* by Owen Wister, and the best-selling book of 1938, *The Yearling* by Marjorie Kinnan Rawlings. These three books, all read when I was fifteen years old, produced my lifelong sense of what it is to be an American. It is not merely that they are set here; they are driven by Americans' love affair with the land. It's different than in the older countries of the world, where the land is taken as a given, a constant. In old countries the land is part of the backdrop of people's lives. It was always there. In America the land is found by each generation, fresh as a bride. We grow up with the land as you grow up with your own family, experiencing its turns of mood and circumstance as you would those of a brother or sister or parent. On this point Hannah and I agreed, even though neither of us had a brother or a sister or a parent.

―――

Y O U never knew what you were going to get for kids in the Enfield school, there was so much coming and going in the Valley. Mainly going. Hannah Corkery wasn't going anywhere, though. She was a state kid, lived at the poor farm in Prescott. She showed up at the school in the fall of 1936.

The farm at Prescott wasn't much, two plain houses with a number of small rooms upstairs, a bunch of outbuildings, and penned-in areas for crops. A dozen folks lived there, including a warden named Honus Hasby, a plump man with owlish eyes and muttonchop whiskers. Honus was supposed to represent the town fathers and the forces of law and discipline. In fact he was the least disciplined of any of the people at the farm. He would sneak up behind any woman, particularly if she was at a chore, and squeeze this or that part of her. Hannah hit him across the forehead with the flat side of a plank when she was eleven. He didn't bother her after that but remained a torment to the older women. They had no one to complain to. They were pretty much soiled doves, soft upstairs or problems with whiskey or men or usually both. Honus would say they were lying. Nobody in town believed them, and nothing was done with Honus.

The three men who lived at the farm were too teched in the head to be much use at the chores, so the women made up the rent to the town fathers by delivering the crops and eggs. Not so different than in the other parts of town.

Hannah was the only child at the poor farm, no kin to anybody there. She never knew who her parents were, so she had had to grow up fast. She had black hair in pigtails, a wide face with freckles, eyes set well apart, a sign of intelligence and more. Except for the color of her hair, she looked somewhat like Little Orphan Annie, the favorite cartoon character of both Uncle Ed and Lawyer Kincaid. Her mouth was too large and her lips too full for the rest of her face. When she smiled, which was often, mouth and lips would be drawn to a proper proportion. You could see both rows of teeth when she smiled.

I liked to look at Hannah and not say anything, just study her, but I wasn't sure what I wanted to find out. There was a gap between the two upper front teeth, and a sizable chip off the right one. She would never tell how her tooth got chipped. That was all right by me. I liked not knowing. I liked not quite knowing, and not quite understanding, things that Hannah knew and understood. I had all the time in the world, I thought.

Hannah threw a ball overhand and could climb a tree faster than most of the boys at the Enfield school. She could throw her head and shoulders off to one side, yet still walk at an ordinary gait, as though she was in a cave or a room with a low ceiling. This amused me, though others found it freakish.

None of the families in town that took boarders would have Hannah. People thought her slow because when she was asked a question, she paused before she spoke. They figured she was gone bad in the head and sent her to the poor farm. Nobody knew where she came from, so nobody objected. Least of all Hannah. "It was a blessing," she told me on her first day at the Enfield school.

"Why was it a blessing?" I asked.

"Because I like to be alone," she said. "Or as alone as I can be."

"How is that?"

"I'm always thinking about people, either the ones I've just been doing things with or ones in the past. Some of the ones in the past, I'm the same person as them."

"But you're you."

She laughed. "At least you think I'm me. The others think I'm nobody."

I shrugged.

Hannah took my forearm in her hand. It was an affectionate gesture, but it alarmed me. It was the gesture of an old woman. I looked at her eyes to see if they had changed, but they were still merry. If there's one thing that sends me moving sideways, it's a look of compassion in another person's eyes. That I don't need. It sets me to thinking and makes me end up feeling worse.

"I have dreams and think about them later," Hannah said. "I have a dream every few weeks where I'm inside a house and it's dark because the windows are slits. The floor is earth. There is noise everywhere, whooping and reports and screaming and moaning, and there's smells of gunpowder and sights of blood and people with arrows and a vacant space off to the side where there's a blur, you can't see anything. I think that's where my little daughter was who carried this memory down into my dreams."

"Your little daughter?"

"I'm the woman handing muskets to the man at the slit window, then cramping the charge back down the barrel of another rifle and handing it back to him. I see everything she sees, I smell everything she smells. There's a blur in the corner, where the girls used to sit."

"The girls?"

"I know I had two daughters, but I never saw them again. My Samuel screamed; he had an arrow just above the clavicle, not mortal but it kept him from firing, so he turned from the window to draw it out. In that moment he had another arrow in the back of the neck, clear through to his Adam's apple. He said nothing, not a sound, mercifully, only fell forward. The first part of him that hit the earth was the arrow point, coming out the front of his neck."

"This is in your dream?"

"I was there. The door slammed open and the space was filled with boys, muscular and naked to the waist. They were covered with paint and shouting, barking without meaning, no more than boys. One of them fell on Samuel and carved out part of his hair with a knife. I've blamed myself that I stood there looking on, didn't fling myself on him. Of course, by that time he was gone and there were two braves holding me."

"Who were you?"

"I never had a name in my dream. Sometimes I heard men talking about 'Oriel,' both before I was captured and after I came back. I think I was Oriel. Not among the Indians, though. There I did have a name. I was Oh-To-Lan, Little Thrush."

"Captured?"

"I lived eleven years among the Nipmucs. The first two were the worst of my life, the middle four or five were the best of my life. The Indians understand the Spirit, the Great Spirit, and they worship by what they do, not what they say. Then I grew apart from my Indian family. After I returned to Dana, I was no closer to the folks there. I was apart from everybody, except the spirits."

"You lived with the Indians and came back to civilization?"

"The Nipmucs were more civilized than the people in Dana, certainly more civilized than the rich people. I was a popular guest for dinner in Dana. People didn't know how to treat me. I was already an old woman, thirty-nine, when I returned. Some people didn't want to let me into their parlors, because they assumed I had been ravished by the braves and were afraid I might communicate something to their furniture. Eventually I was married off, against my wishes and judgment, to Alfred Woolsey. I finished up as Mrs. Alfred Woolsey."

"Who were you married off by, if it was against your wishes? Who could force you?"

"It wasn't physical force. It was an assumption on the part of everybody in the town, an assumption that was as good as force. No one would deal with you in any way except based on the assumption. I refused to admit Alfred to my bed, confirming his worst suspicions. Even though the suspicions were false.

"People in Dana overlooked a lot for me, though. The Valley had no entertainments or news of the outside world. People lived on work and love alone, and many had no love."

"You were their entertainment?"

"All I had to do was sit there. I was like a two-headed cow, didn't have to say anything to get people's full attention, and have them be grateful, in a way."

"Was it worth it?"

"Not a bit. Being pushed around by other people's assumptions means you don't get to live your own life."

"It can be your life even if other people expect it. I'm expected to till my family's fields, to stay in the Valley. I expect I shall. That will be my choice, so it will be my life."

"Will it? I'd rather lead other lives, lives no one can see and complain about. So I have."

"Has that been your choice?"

"I've just been lucky."

I laughed. "You make things boring when you're not around," I said.

———

———

My classmate Caleb Durand was a rawboned boy, with fine blond hair, a high hairline, green eyes, and a thin mouth. He looked to have just stepped off a Viking ship. From his appearance you would guess he would be austere in deportment. He was the opposite: sloppy, jolly, disorganized. If he claimed he could not come along on an adventure because of chores or schoolwork, all you had to say was, "Come on!" and he would be out the door before you.

Caleb's father was a big man, Mr. Durand to me, a foreman at the grain mill. He seemed to care only for his work, at which he was concededly efficient. His great-uncle Robert had for a time led the Hatfields against the McCoys in their border feud in West Virginia and Kentucky. I was certain that Mr. Durand must have a cache of rifles somewhere on his property.

Caleb's mother was a sparrowlike creature with brown eyes, dark freckles, and masses of lovely curls that dwarfed her frame. Her name was Missy. She spoke little but loved Caleb openly.

Caleb and I lived to get beneath the surface, whether it was land or water. We used to dive in the quarry pool. Two teenagers had found a body in an underwater cave there a few years earlier. The cold water and limestone had perfectly preserved the features. It was old Ed Sawyer, wedged into a sitting position and grinning at you like he was about to stick out his hand and say howdy. Sawyer had had a huge row with his brother-in-law over some woman, and word was there had been a knife fight in the big barn at Atherton's place in Smith's Village, but he had not been found, even though the trail of his blood led right into the woods.

The brother-in-law was never tried for anything. Right after the detectives announced they couldn't find the body, the brother-in-law married the woman. So she couldn't testify, by law, and the only other witness was dead.

Once we were floating down Egypt Brook, past a curve in the shoreline piled high with sticks, and found an opening in the mud bank, four feet underwater. Caleb ran out of breath the first two times he tried to get through to explore the passage, so I said I would take a turn, as I can hold my breath well over a minute underwater. That's what saved me years later in the North Atlantic.

I wriggled through the opening and found the passage. It led not into the bank but upward. I was about to back out, to allow time to return to the surface, when my head broke out of water into an unlit space. Instantly there were explosions on the surface around me. I felt something bulky and something sharp push past my feet. I thought I was done for, and gasped for air, even though there was no shortage.

"Caleb, help!" I screamed. This was the first and only time in my life I have ever screamed for help, including when I was hurled into the freezing ocean at night. I blush to recall it. It seems so predictable.

I heard Caleb from close by but far away: "You're inside a beaver hutch, you fool!"

This experience was more terrifying than anything I saw in wartime.

Nobody was as at home in the tunnels as Caleb and I were. Some of these had been dug for the railroads, the Rabbit north-south and the abandoned east-west line. Some were spurs off the big Wachusett tunnel, or diversions from the spillway area at Winsor Locks. Some were connected to the open mine areas: quartz, gravel, soapstone, and lime. At the end, I bet Lawyer Kincaid wished he had spent less time reading up on how to bankrupt poor farmers and more time studying up on those tunnels.

At the Hastings mine in Greenwich, Caleb and I found a side shaft, deep underground, sealed off by a pile of boulders. We came back the next day with a lantern and moved the rocks one at a time, careful so as not to provoke a slide, until we had created a space we could get through. I was first into the opening, wriggling on my stomach and reaching my fingers out to probe the floor and ceiling of the crawl space. Caleb had the lantern behind me, so it didn't show me any light. The first thing I touched, I knew it was all wrong. It wasn't pebbles, it wasn't a dirt floor, didn't seem to be part of the place. It proved to be a denim shirt, with an arm bone in it. The man had been stretching out his fingers, just like mine, scratching at the pile caused by the cave-in. Turned out to be five skeletons, with their clothes still on, stacked on top of one another like rocks, right up against the rubble. Must have been gasping for air.

Uncle Ed didn't hesitate. He was excited, said it was the Hastings mining disaster, sixty years ago, and they were the five Polish workers, good, hard workers, all Protestants, who were never found.

From my first memories as a boy in the Valley, well before I ever met Hannah Corkery, I was certain of one thing: the dead were all around us.

———

———

M̲ᴇɴ had had grand plans for the Swift River Valley.
Shortly after the turn of the century, a handsome Italian
industrialist named Gebetti raised a fantastic sum of money
in the drawing rooms of Beacon Hill and the Back Bay in
Boston, to finance the construction of an east-west railroad
that would have gone right through Ware and Greenwich.
Apparently in constructing a rail line the trick is to do the
hard parts first, so as fast as the money was raised, it was
poured into blasting whatever hill or mountain lay in the
path of the oncoming Central Mass. Railroad. The idea was
you would hook up all the tunnels later.

Word was that Mr. Gebetti went bankrupt before the job
could be finished; what was certain was that after a series of
frantic calls for capital, he returned to Europe and was not
seen again in Boston. Better for him, as that is where his
bondholders lived.

Had he wished, old Gebetti could have had a hero's welcome among the children of Ware, Greenwich, and Enfield.
His legacy was a chain of hollowed-out hills, of ditches and
trenches and cave-ins, tracks and ties laid down, torn up, and
cast aside, a playground hospitable and nonthreatening, yet
vast and beyond our power to create.

The abandoned ties became tree houses and clubhouses,
the abandoned tunnels and cave-ins hosted illicit fires, dangerous dares, daylong games of hide-and-seek.

The crown jewels in the chain were two engines, one sunk
deep in a swamp in Greenwich, the other wedged into a
stand of birch four miles west of Ware. How they had come
to these states of repose was a mystery; neither one was with-

in half a mile of the planned route for the track. My judgment was that "train robbers"—a band to whom I had been introduced through a pamphlet of Tom Mix comic cartoons—must have dropped the engines in haste while being pursued by a "posse" (ditto).

The superstructure of the Greenwich engine was still accessible, so it became the Confederate garrison at Vicksburg, on the Mississippi; boats and rafts of Union soldiers armed with water balloons were poled past it during the night. While the garrison was always overrun, to be in command of that much steel was the most prized position in our Civil War games.

The engine in Ware was something else. Nine months of the year its stack still belched smoke into the air, visible day and night if you stepped back from the woods. The engine made no headway; it was inhabited by Hammy the hobo, who kept that fire burning and had held his citadel against all comers for so long that any effort to dislodge him had been abandoned.

Hammy was probably not over forty years of age but had only a few good teeth still in him. His hair and his eyes went every which way. None of us knew when or whence he had taken up his locomotive residence. To us he was a sultan, not a squatter.

Hammy looked and moved like a bear. His body and clothes were generally sooty. His face was white, almost shiny, for he scrubbed in the stream every morning and evening. Not particular as to the general conditions of life, in small things Hammy was as fastidious as a raccoon.

Hammy walked in a crouch. In an hour's hunt through the forest, he could find half a dozen quartz arrowheads from the time of King Philip's War where Caleb and I could not see a one. I am sure it was his eyesight and long habit; he, how-ever, insisted that his lineage ran straight to the Wampa-noag tribe of Massasoit, so that this was an inherited talent. Certainly Hammy had retained the pride of a dying culture; though I suppose, in truth, the Indians were no longer fight-ing on, except in my attic.

Hammy could move on ground strewn with sticks and dry leaves without making a sound. More than once while I stood sentry duty in military operations in his woods, he came up behind me to within two feet of my position and popped a handful of Indian puffballs between his palms. I died many deaths as a sentry; I was fortunate eventually to find other work.

Hammy's body had absorbed a few blows. He seemed to have a limp, though you could not have said which leg. It was only that he moved across land with a kind of dipping motion.

His right arm had an occasional jerk, or tic, though if he was extending a palm for you to inspect and compare six species of mushrooms from the woods, there would be no tremor. He could catch any kind of snake by pinching the back of its neck with his right hand, at the same time gather-ing the lower portion of its body in his left so it could not escape by thrashing about. I grew used to this, but when Hammy snuck up behind a coiled timber rattler that was hissing at me and Caleb, even I was impressed.

The wallpaper of Hammy's home was a substantial yellow birch, against which the engine rested at a slight angle. Over the years the cinders had burned through many layers of the

———

trunk and a large overhanging branch. The tree had sealed off these deep wounds and grown around them. Birches are tougher than their reputation. Still not as tough as a beech, but they don't have as much raw material to work with.

Hammy was a hobo but far from a hermit. For a person who had chosen to live off to the side, he had quite a social impulse. He moved freely through the five towns during the day and had a nodding acquaintance with most everybody in them. He never bought anything and never begged. He often had things from the woods to give to the youngsters: an odd knot of wood, a perfect nest, a fungus, a small tangle of berries and vines, occasionally an arrowhead. Toward the grown-ups he was uniformly respectful, even if a few of them did make a point of crossing the street to avoid him.

He became a favorite of Grandma because of his kindness toward the children, particularly little Pudge Mullally, who had a difficult time at home. Grandma learned after one try not to offer Hammy money for anything. He would always take a bite of shortbread or a book on loan, though. After he showed her his copy of *Walden,* by Henry David Thoreau, she lent him a set of essays by Nietzsche, the philosopher. He kept it for two months. Grandma told me she suspected Hammy had had more education than he admitted.

W H I L E almost nobody in the Valley had an automobile, except for the mill and shop owners, we children had our own private transportation system, the Rabbit Railroad. Hammy, who had evidently had some history riding the rails in the

---

West in his youth, encouraged us to use the Rabbit. It ran north-south through the whole Valley, from Athol to Palmer, making nineteen stops along the way, two round trips every day. The engineer was a persnickety gent who called himself Phineas Neptune. I don't think either was his real name. If he saw somebody he knew at any station, he would tarry up to twenty minutes to pass the time of day. There was a printed schedule somewhere for the Rabbit Railroad, but nobody used it because it wouldn't help you at all.

We didn't care. We had all morning, or all afternoon, to wait; and if there was a long stop, it meant only that there was more time to sneak on board, between cars. Old Phineas knew exactly what we were doing, but he never looked at us, never let on that he saw us. Except once, little Pudge Mullally was between two cars when the coupling came loose, or at least started to rattle, and you never saw anyone move so fast as old Phineas Neptune.

Hammy introduced us to the twelve-mile aqueduct from Ware to the Wachusett Reservoir, which the Water Supply Commission had constructed in the 1920s. A couple of miles east of Ware, the aqueduct was paralleled for a mile by a twin tunnel, a false start that had been given up for some reason of geology or engineering. Both tunnels had side shafts, some holding active pumping equipment and others partially caved in and abandoned. The whole area, said Hammy, had been loose stones left by a glacier, which made footing and tunneling equally treacherous. The glacier had stretched from northern New Hampshire to Long Island Sound. Hammy said it melted a million years ago, dumping its talus in Massachusetts and creating a flood that filled a five-mile lake in Connecticut. I never heard that story from anyone else, until I met a geologist on board my ship in the North Atlantic and he said it was true.

———

IT took a long time for it to sink in on the townspeople what was coming. Hard to come to terms with your world being obliterated, I suppose. You'd rather think about something else, some task right before you. The people in the Valley did, anyway. Nor was I an exception.

In 1927, when I was four years old, the legislature in Boston passed a law to authorize the taking of all the property in the Valley. The representatives from western Massachusetts voted against it, but they were badly outnumbered by the legislators from Boston and its suburbs.

There wasn't much worrying for several years. Lawyer Kincaid kept telling folks that it was never going to happen, that he could stop it, that sentiment in Boston was mixed, that they would roll it back. Grandma asked him if he thought he could roll back the waters of the Swift River. Most of the other townsfolk took him at his word.

It wasn't real to me until one evening in October 1937. I was standing on a hill in Prescott with Hannah, opposite Mount Pomeroy. We were watching a pair of eagles take the wind.

"That looks like fun," she said.

"Yes."

"They mate for life, you know."

"I know." I had just turned fifteen, and doubted there was much anyone could tell me that I didn't know. I dropped my

———

head. I saw a man driving a team of oxen, slow, against the blue dusk. Up above was a roof interrupting the treeline of a hill. Man's influence, in the right proportion: only a flourish, a signature. The blue was deep, all movement was slow, all sound was muted. It was the most beautiful scene.

"Do you smell that?" she asked.

"Smell what?"

She pointed to the foot of Pomeroy. There were three plumes of smoke from fires made of cut trees and an old shack. Hannah later said that was the memory most stamped on her: the smell of smoke throughout the Valley, from the houses and trees that had been bulldozed and cut to pieces.

I didn't at first perceive what could be the horror of smoke. Smoke had drifted through my life, generally representing the impending arrival of something good to eat or a corner of warmth against the chill of a gray day outside. I loved to watch the chimney smoke from the Durands' cabin in the dell curling upside down for hours, held by the inversion in the air of the hollow. Caleb and I would beat at it with alder poles, and it would still hang there, white and ugly as a possum.

The smoke that Hannah and I smelled that day was different. It had the scent of nails in it, of tar and mortar and other fixings you'd never put in a fire to warm you or cook you food. Not like the smoke of my boyhood. It was insistent rather than lazy, an intruder rather than a presence. I came to see what Hannah meant.

———

———

THAT same month, Caleb and I were walking in the wild part of Prescott with our slingshots, to find what we could. The red maples, the locusts, and the ash were well on their way to turning, the sugar maples and birch not far behind. The oak and the beech so far would have none of it: they wait till November before bowing to the fall fashion.

For a while we amused ourselves by throwing acorns at each other and ducking behind trees. Then we came on a trail of hair balls: warm coyote scat. We plunged along a little ridge and soon sighted the animal. Caleb let fly with a rock the size of his thumb and was rewarded with a *ki-yi-yi* of pain. The coyote took off lickety-split with us in pursuit, then vanished as though plucked by a hand from below. We ran up and found the miserable animal had fallen six feet into the cellar hole of a razed farmhouse. Worse for him, he was not alone, having interrupted the slumber of a fisher-cat who had been sunning himself on the raised hearth. A fisher-cat doesn't look like much, sort of a drab overgrown otter, but you don't want to interrupt them at anything.

The coyote, remembering he was a predator, arched his shoulders and snarled. The hair on his back bristled from neck to tail as he advanced on the smaller creature. He must have been full of confidence.

Caleb made his eyes wide. I understood: inch for inch and pound for pound, there is no more savage adversary in all the natural world than the fisher-cat. One of them will kill twenty porcupines.

For an instant the fisher-cat appeared almost to smile at the coyote. Like porcupines and rabbits, fishers have teeth with circulating blood; they are not dead matter like ours. His fangs were a deep ivory color, almost orange. It seemed the coyote's lifeblood already filled his mouth.

We had not long to wait. The coyote went for the fisher-cat as he slipped off the hearthstones, and succeeded in grabbing his hindquarters in his maw. The fisher-cat broke free with a single rounding twist, in the same motion clawing the side of the coyote's head into strings of flesh. The coyote stumbled about the cellar, but there was no exit. The cat darted up behind and under him, tearing his throat apart with a swipe of his fangs. The coyote rolled onto his side, his tongue in the dirt, his eyes sideways.

The fisher-cat looked up at us as we were drawing a bead with our slingshots, made a calculation, and darted into a crevice in the cellar wall, invisible to the human eye and too small for the godforsaken coyote even had he been in the best of health.

For no reason but to mark the occasion with solemnity, Caleb and I threw down brush to cover the coyote. He was stone dead, no blood gushing from his terrible wounds. I say threw down—we loved the netherworld, but not a pot of gold would have tempted us to descend to the floor of the cellar hole. Those crevices might have held forty fisher-cats, all drooling crimson.

When things are covered over, whether it's the woods reclaiming fields or waters reclaiming a valley, human savagery is replaced by nature's savagery. Or nature's indifference. Either way it's an improvement. I'll take the fisher-cat or the badger, the weasel or the wolverine; you can have Lawyer Kincaid and his little ways.

———

Y E A R S later I heard people from Boston say that the taking of our land and the flooding of the five towns never could have happened if there hadn't been the Depression, if people hadn't become so dependent on the government. This was rubbish. In the hill towns we had no idea there was a government, except in the towns. We suffered the fancy state judges to come and sit in superior court once every six months, but as soon as they were gone no one paid any attention to what they had decided. When we learned that civil engineers can do you more harm than judges, it was too late.

My strongest memories of the late 1930s have nothing to do with the Depression or Prohibition or Adolf Hitler or President Roosevelt or even Seabiscuit. They have to do with catching bullheads at night with a string, a pin, and earthworms from behind the barn. The time I shot a cottontail in the eye with my slingshot and it raced around me in circles for a full minute before it died. Finding Indian arrowheads down the lane, pink-and-white quartz. Feeling the heat in summer, raising your neck for a breeze, watching the paint blister, following the black-and-white hornets so we could burn their nest, dodging the yellow jackets, swimming in Egypt Brook. Hiking up Petersham Hill in the fall, picking ferns and wildflowers, filling a bag with chestnuts for roasting.

It was a wonder life. How were we to believe our fellow citizens of Massachusetts were about to chop down every tree and bulldoze every home in the Valley?

———

Fall

GRANDMA Hardiman and I had a good life on the farm. In her fifties, she was still fit. Miss Ettie Clark, an assistant schoolteacher in the Enfield school, lived in our back room and shared the household chores. Miss Ettie had lovely long hair, reddish blond. She usually wore it up, in a bun. She had a soft voice.

A handyman, Francis Perrault, lived in a room above the horses' stalls in the barn. He had weather-beaten skin, a thin mustache already gone partly gray, and a wary look, a squint, as though he had spent years on the deck of a ship. I loved the smell of his room: manure, hay, and tobacco.

Francis had showed up at the place on foot, said he had walked all the way from Providence, Rhode Island. Fools'

Island, Lawyer Kincaid called it, because their legislature always sided with the farmers, since the time of Captain Shays. Grandma, being a farmer in her bones, thought Rhode Island a kind of heaven.

"Why did you ever leave, Francis?" she asked one Sunday at supper, when we were sharing a platter of eggs and beans.

The question seemed to disconcert Francis. When Miss Ettie got up at that moment to clear dishes, the screech of her chair on the floorboards seemed louder than usual. Francis patted his mouth with his napkin, giving a small cough behind the napkin.

"There was no real reason, ma'am," he said, coughing again. "No particular reason." He looked around and saw this wouldn't do, given that he had arrived without notice or possessions.

"Except that, I truly wasn't *from* there." Everyone nodded and relaxed. Francis smiled at his escape. Then he decided to explain further.

"I was raised in Quebec Province, in Canada."

"How is your French?" asked Uncle Ed. The tension settled back over the room. Miss Ettie left the dishes to dry and slipped upstairs.

"I wasn't from that part of Quebec," said Francis, setting his napkin on the table in a show of finality. He rose and stepped into the room behind the kitchen. He stood by the big sink with the washboard and nudged the butter churn to one side with his knee. He drew the ice pick off its nail, opened the door of the icebox, and with four quick thrusts produced a single piece of ice the size of a jar. With this in hand he stepped out back, taking care not to let the screen door slam.

Uncle Ed looked at Grandma. "Frenchman, eh?" he said. "I'd say more likely he's got a touch of the tar brush in him."

"What does that mean?" I said.

"Nothing, son," said Grandma.

Uncle Ed lit his pipe.

W E had three horses, a team of oxen, two cows, a goat, and a donkey. With all that, our main crop, if you can believe it, was ice. We cut it from the ponds and dragged and railed it all the way north to Athol and as far east as Palmer, to sell to the shopkeepers and mill and factory owners.

We had a lot of the root crops, of course, parsnips and turnips and beets as well as carrots and potatoes, because nature stored those for you and they filled the belly nicely. On the vine we had beans and peas. We would hang the vines whole on the barn walls in winter; it was a kid's job, my job, to thresh only so much as we needed for the day's meals. "You're my little thresher," Grandma said to me once, patting me on the head. I watched her smile disappear.

Our best field was probably the big oat field, but most of them were set in corn. We were careful with the stalks, as they made fine fodder for the animals, and from the rest we made cornmeal. We would make scrapple out of cornmeal mush by adding lard—we didn't have bacon—thus producing something akin to salt pork. We had that for breakfast on

Sunday, with molasses. I never ate corn on the cob 'til I moved to Pelham. It would have seemed a waste.

There was no radio in our house. You were aware of right where you lived. I knew every tree on the property by its first name, knew every year which branch would produce the best apples or peaches, knew where the huckleberries were thinning and where they would be coming back stronger.

The seasons channel all my memories of those days. You have a stronger sense of temperature and smell when you're young. Those things vary with the time of year.

Every fall we traded in our fishing poles for slingshots— hickory or ash carved into a Y shape, with an elastic band of rubber attached to the top posts. As we got older we acquired facility with longer and stronger bands. By the time I was fifteen I could propel a rock an inch and a half in diameter over a distance of thirty yards with deadly force. We shot dove out of hickory trees, we shot squirrels out of thick elms covered forty feet up with ivy. Once I hit a red fox behind the ear at over fifty yards. He dropped dead as the stone that hit him. His pelt fetched us only three dollars instead of the usual five, as it was mangy. Caleb said he had probably been about to drop dead anyway.

The calendar said the seasons changed in September, but the marker in our household was Thanksgiving. You didn't dare leave a rowboat in a pond after Thanksgiving, or it would be there till the spring, likely with cracks in the hull. That dividing line was more real than the fall solstice.

Turkeys were hard to come by in the hill towns in those days, though Lord knows they are plentiful today. We generally were able to put our hands on a goose or two, as the locals were not fastidious about hunting seasons and bag limits established by the legislature in Boston. Grandma would make a fine corn pudding with cream and bread crumbs, and sweet potatoes with marshmallow. We always had our own Concord grape jelly and blackberry preserve. It was a meal you could look forward to for months.

In 1937 it seemed half the government officials in the Valley were invited to our table. Uncle Ed had arranged for Carl Kincaid, the attorney who was our elected representative to the Great and General Court, and Charles Moncrieff, the new preacher at the Congregational church in Ripton, to come by for cider before the meal, to discuss the status of matters at the State House in Boston. He said he thought Grandma could "benefit from their perspective." She pursed her lips at this. Grandma thought the towns could be saved.

When I came in from morning chores Uncle Ed and Lawyer Kincaid were sitting in the kitchen discussing the upcoming marriage of a North Dana couple.

"He divorced Jessie because she drove him crazy about everything, and now he's hitching up with about the strongest-minded woman in the Valley," said Uncle Ed.

Lawyer Kincaid said, "He's making the same mistake twice, you're right about that, Ed."

"More like, he's still got the same faults that cost him before," said Grandma from the stove.

There was a knock, and the dark outline of Preacher Moncrieff filled the door. The sun was behind him and at first I could not see his face. He stepped in, *clomp-clomp*. He was a large man with enormous hands and a skin disease that covered his neck in purple. It was difficult to imagine him as a boy, or even as a young man.

"I've just been to the Lithcotts," he said. "Barney's not got long, I'm afraid, and Mabel's not in all that much better shape."

"Take off your coat, Preacher," said Grandma. He settled with difficulty into the rocker in the corner and accepted a cider.

"How are you?" Grandma asked him. "You seem a little beaten down, for a strapping fellow like you."

Moncrieff took a sip of cider, puffed out his cheeks, and swooshed it around in his mouth, then swallowed and looked up. "Sometimes I'm not sure, Mrs. Hardiman," he said. "The Valley is an odd area, after Worcester. For most of last month, all anyone seemed to think about was planning for Halloween. Witches, ghosts, skeletons, goblins—the whole thing perfectly calculated to disturb people's understanding of the relationship between life and death. It's all but a celebration of Satan."

"I was a goblin," I said.

Preacher Moncrieff offered me a smile. He raised his arm to pat me on the head, then saw this would be inappropriate. I had grown five inches that year and stood almost six feet tall—nothing like his size, but too far grown to treat as a child. He patted my shoulder instead.

"That's fine, son, you're not the one organizing pagan ceremonies barely in advance of All Souls' Day. When I made my rounds the only souls I saw on porches were twisted corpses."

"Pagan ceremonies?" asked Grandma. "Well, I declare. And who is the one who was organizing Halloween? I'd like to meet that man, put him in charge of organizing to save our towns." Uncle Ed coughed.

"Lawyer Kincaid says there's still hope the men in Boston may choose another plan," said Uncle Ed. Grandma turned toward Kincaid, who shifted in his seat.

"We will, of course, do all in our power," he said.

"Of course, that's it, isn't it?" said the preacher, wheezing and wiping his mouth with a handkerchief. "There's only so much that's within our power."

"The good Lord may have made the Swift River," said Grandma, gesturing with the stirring spoon, "but I doubt very much he has any near-term intentions to dam it by himself. That would require an army of beavers like unto the battalions of the Israelites."

Preacher Moncrieff did not seem amused at the use of the Bible for political argument. "While we're on earth, we have a world to run out there," he said.

"Spoken like a true politician," said Uncle Ed. Kincaid nodded.

"Caesar had an army to run," said Grandma, "and when his soldiers fared poorly in battle he would line them up on parade and behead every tenth man, irrespective of whether he had fought bravely."

"His armies were rather successful," said Kincaid.

"That doesn't mean we need to adopt his methods," said Grandma. "A world to run is not a world to ruin."

"Of course not," said Lawyer Kincaid. He finished his cider, set down his glass, rose, tipped his hat, and departed.

———

"Didn't say good-bye," observed Uncle Ed.

"That's the only part I appreciated," said Grandma. "They say, 'Don't complain, don't explain, never apologize.' I agree with that, and also try to avoid saying 'please,' 'hello,' 'good-bye,' or 'thank you.'"

The preacher laughed. "Why is that? I thought 'please' and 'thank you' were magic words."

"So I was taught as a little girl, but I soon learned that 'thank you' is not a magic word, because nothing happens when you say 'thank you.'"

Uncle Ed grimaced at this but the preacher laughed and poured himself another cider.

A knock at the back screen door announced the arrival of Hammy the hobo. I was startled that he had presumed on my friendship to stop by unannounced on such a day, but Grandma told him to come right in. She introduced him to Uncle Ed and to Preacher Moncrieff, who took his filthy hand with some hesitancy. His eye fell to Hammy's tattered and outsized moccasins.

"That's a substantial pair of brogues you have there," he said.

"Takes a wider foundation to hold up a church than an outhouse," said Hammy. Moncrieff winced.

"It's all right, Hammy's descended from the Wampanoags, don't you see?" said Grandma. "I mean, under the circumstances . . ." Uncle Ed was staring at the floor.

"It's Thanksgiving!" said Grandma. "The Indians were our hosts, Ed, for goodness' sake. Remember the first Thanksgiving." She passed around a plate of shortbread, which was a twice-a-year delicacy. "Remember what my grandmother always said: 'Look long, finger them all, and take the biggest!'"

"Yes, ma'am," said Hammy, helping himself first. Now Moncrieff and Uncle Ed were both studying the floor. There was bad feeling in the room. Grown-ups are funny, I thought, and took two pieces of shortbread.

"That's a good boy, Jamieson," said Grandma. "Worldly pleasure is sacred."

Moncrieff left a few moments later. He said good-bye to every person in the room and did not put on his hat till he was out the door.

"You were a bit rough on him, a man of the cloth and a new neighbor," said Uncle Ed.

"My sense is he can take care of himself," said Grandma. "Hsst, Ettie, come in here and have some shortbread."

Miss Ettie, who had been passing by the hallway door, entered the room a step and curtsied to Grandma. "Thank you so kindly, Mrs. Hardiman, I'm going just now to join Sal Foster and Millie Tiverton for the noon meal, at the Foster place, and I dare not spoil my appetite. You're very kind, they do look delicious."

"Off with you, then," said Grandma. As soon as Ettie was out of the house she turned to Uncle Ed, who was staring at the fire.

"That girl has better natural manners than if she had spent her entire born life doing nothing but rehearse 'Papa, prunes, and prisms,'" she said.

Uncle Ed shook his head slowly from side to side. "If you say so," he said.

———

———

Our house was drab, green-and-gray wood that gave play to the wind through gaps in the siding. The ground floor did not detain children long: front room to the left, dining room on the right, kitchen beyond. These were adult spaces. Even the kitchen with its raised hearth was too much a place of authority for us.

The second floor held Grandma's room in front, my small bedroom, a sewing and sitting parlor, and Miss Ettie's room in the back. The second-floor rooms had been ruined by successful attempts to feminize them through dainty wallpaper and lace, lace everywhere. Every stick of furniture had two or three antimacassars draped over it; you didn't dare touch anything.

The third floor was the attic, real property abandoned by those in power. Everything was a mess, corridors between piles of lumber, here a wall and a door for no reason, there an abandoned sink or tub, here a seagoing chest with broken hasp, there old newspapers, here stuffed birds or dolls, there a trapdoor, here a cradle, there a hidden compartment, an empty room with a window but no electricity.

For me and Caleb, the attic was heaven.

In a corner of the empty room I kept my collection of hand-painted cowboys and Indians, plaster over their wire cores. There were no replicas of Captain Shays's men, nor General Lincoln's, so the cowboys and Indians served as my window on the military world.

Like real-life soldiers they had to complete their maneu-

———

vers during daylight hours, for when darkness overcame them they could not move: I could not see to pick them up for their next advance.

Of the provenance of these figures I have no idea, but they were fashioned with some skill. The Indians, dressed in rags, had drawn, gaunt faces and haunted eyes—incomparably more savage than the cowboys, who were creaseless in costume and complexion, resembling the models in newspaper advertisements for dough or paint.

If ever there were fair and equal fights among stick figures, it was among these soldiers. There were twenty-eight Indians and twenty-four cowboys, including two unarmed men whose only function was to sit atop a wooden stagecoach drawn by four piebalds. One of these carried a whip but the other did not, having been literally unarmed by decades of rough use. (I was not the original proprietor of any of this matériel.) So it was really twenty-eight to twenty-two, though the cowboys had a greater number of carbines. Many of the natives relied on tomahawks and headdresses to terrify their foe.

The tide of battle invariably surged from side to side, devolving to the last man left standing, who would then be shot by a surreptitious and gravely wounded adversary. Generally the last two combatants died simultaneously, continuing the symmetry of previous casualties. At that point I would rise to my feet, to survey the bloody field from an Olympian perspective. It did look different, I have to say.

In another corner of the large room, underneath the skylight, I maintained my workshop. This contained many bits of bark and wood, both natural and hewn, a substantial quantity of string and twine, a needle, thimble and thread, a small hammer, assorted nails—very much assorted—and from somewhere a sawhorse, which balanced, supported, and interdicted nothing. The function of the sawhorse was to announce to whoever might intrude that this was a professional work area.

In this space I played endlessly with colored string wound around twigs. Such an artifact could triple in brass as a log in flames, a sofa of high fashion, or a miniature papoose. As a papoose, an orange-wrapped twig occupied the center of my magnificent canoe: a foot-long stretch of hollowed oak, wrapped along the exterior with white birch sewn on yellow birch. The thwarts were twigs of maple, the gunwales sprigs of cedar. The bow was occupied by a joyous dough-faced cowboy, eyes and armament trained before him; the stern, by a slinking, mauve-chested native, clad only in green buckskins, tomahawk at the ready.

————

USING my workshop, Caleb had carved a gunboat out of balsam, fashioned after the ironsides of the War Between the States. It had an eclectic battery on either side: twelve nails, no two alike, supplied the firepower.

On most Sunday afternoons we raced our craft against each other on French King Brook, cheering them on over open courses, howling when they became stuck in an eddy or caught on an overhanging branch. The winner got to keep the losing vessel for the next week.

The competition ended in tragedy. After a heavy October

————

rain we misjudged the speed of the current in the brook's longest straightaway. We dallied too long at a best-of-seven series of mumblety-peg by the Great Rock. When we looked up, both boats were two hundred yards downstream, under heavy steam. We could not catch up with them before the waterfall over the Great Pool. Neither one emerged from the foam at the bottom of the falls. We dove for an hour, but that pool is twenty feet deep in places and not without submerged trees, so finally we had to give it up. Each of us had only one consolation: that the other's prize possession had also been lost.

———

THE town fathers of Prescott had paid to send Hannah Corkery to the Enfield school. They thought perhaps Ettie Clark could help this obviously troubled youngster. Miss Ettie was known to be gentle with people.

After a few months Miss Ettie reported to the town fathers of Prescott and Enfield that while Hannah was uncommonly dreamy, she seemed to possess an accurate store of knowledge as to the architecture, clothing, habits, and vocabulary of the Swift River Valley towns in the eighteenth century.

This was laid down to Hannah's always poring over old books that no one else would read. A book was found in a box in the Prescott town library, containing a description of the 1765 farm of Samuel and Oriel Twynham that matched Hannah's account in most details. It was concluded that Hannah must have found the book and committed the description to memory.

———

It did not disturb Hannah in the slightest that she was disbelieved. "This gives me more room to move around," she told me.

Like me, Hannah was an indifferent student at the school. She said she had difficulty paying attention to the present, an assertion confirmed by Miss Clark. After school, I would listen to her tell about life on the Twynham farm during the Indian wars, or the tragic romance she had had with one of Captain Shays's men at the time of the insurrection, or her brief and unhappy experience as Kathleen Connley, a star-crossed lover just after the War Between the States.

Adults paid no attention to Hannah's historical descriptions, but they were troubled by her talking about the "presences" on the poor farm—meaning the dead people—and how Clara was here last night, or Virgil or Henry, and how they walked together through the orchard, and everything was shining at midnight as though there were a thousand candles ringing the field.

Hannah did walk in her sleep, and even talk, but folks wouldn't let it go at that. They had to say she was a liar.

I knew why they did it. Everybody on Prescott Peninsula had seen lights and shimmering around the houses on nights with no moon; most everybody had felt presences in their beds and could tell whether it was a man or a woman and whether young or old. Two grown-ups told me they had seen men and women in formal dress dancing in the barn at Lithcott's on Thanksgiving night, the whole room pulsing with light and music. The next morning nothing was there. But I wasn't to tell anybody, on no account.

———

Folks didn't like hearing from Hannah what they knew was true but weren't allowed to admit to one another.

These incidents—the sightings—got more frequent as the 1930s went by. There was a rash of reports when the men from the Water Supply Commission began digging up the graveyards to transplant the deaders, in preparation for the flooding. Uncle Ed said it was done because the dead bodies wouldn't be good for the water quality once the Valley was flooded. But it seemed to me nobody likes being disturbed in that way, dead or alive. It didn't strike me odd that the spirits would go abroad around their old homes in all the towns, not just Prescott.

———

EVERY Sunday morning without fail Grandma and I went in for the other kind of spirits, trekking to local Congregational services. At the beginning of her second year at the Enfield school, Hannah began to ask me questions about the church services: where did people sit and stand, when were they quiet and when did they sing out, did the parishioners talk back to the preacher, and so on. One day she asked if she could accompany us to services that Sunday.

"You don't believe a word of this," I said.

"I want to see how the congregants react to the sermon," she said, "as the fire and brimstone engulfs them."

Until Preacher Moncrieff came to the Valley we had pretty much stuck to the Enfield church, but now every few weeks Grandma would forsake the mild-mannered reverend Cecil

Wray and take us to hear Moncrieff at Ripton. I reckoned it was because he was the only soul in the Valley who had read more books than Grandma. She told me and Hannah, over a Sunday morning wedge of apple pie and slice of cheddar, it was not his erudition.

"I'm curious. There's something wrong there. Charles Moncrieff is an intelligent man, well educated, has traveled a lot, has lived in the Carolinas and in France. He has personal force, not just the force of his convictions. He seems bigger than he is, which is plenty big. But look at his eyes when he's not preaching: he's aching for something. I want to find out what it is."

"Do you think it's something religious, Grandma?"

"That's the interesting part. I rather doubt it. He seems to have his teachings nailed down pretty squarely within four corners. There's no mystery there, and not much opening for change."

"Are you surprised he chose the church as a profession?" said Hannah.

"It's highly respected in the community." Grandma's eyes twinkled as she said this.

"Perhaps it was not his first choice," said Hannah.

Without a word Grandma walked over and kissed Hannah on the side of her head, by her eye. Hannah must have seen what was coming, but made no move to resist. They remained in this posture for some seconds, as though Grandma's lips were transmitting some currency to Hannah's eye, or perhaps the reverse. I froze in my place.

Grandma broke the spell. "Right you are," she said, touching Hannah on the shoulder. "Now we must be off, or we'll miss the opening fulmination."

Moncrieff was in a sour mood that day, though to be fair, the Bennetts' beagle barked outside the church throughout the service. The instruction to the congregants seemed to be twofold: first, if things were not good, that was of our own doing; and second, it was our bounden duty to submit to the order of things, which had been arranged by a Higher Power.

We stayed in our pew while the others were filing out, so that Grandma could have Preacher Moncrieff to herself at the end of the line.

"I love sermons," said Hannah happily. "A Higher Power did it, and it's our fault."

"I must say, something of the same thought had occurred to me," said Grandma, sighing as she rose to leave. Grandma was the least submitting person I ever met. At the back of the church she took the miserable preacher's hand in both of hers and would not let go.

"Now, Charles, can't we work on a more *constructive* message for next week? Perhaps a guide to action of some sort, rather than a guide to inaction?"

Moncrieff was eyeing the beagle, which had now waddled through the back door of the church and was ominously sniffing the side of a pew. With some effort he turned his attention back to Grandma.

"To transmit the Word of the Lord, to the best of one's ability, is not commonly viewed as unhelpful." He gave her a smile. "At least in my line of work."

"No, I suppose not," said Grandma. "Not in your line of

work." She let his hand go, and we moved on. When we were halfway up the hill there was a frightful yowl from the beagle.

———

Pudge Mullally, the son of our science teacher, was seven years younger than I was, so he was a mascot for me and Caleb and Hannah. He had big black eyes, wide with wonder, and I got a kick out of him, as the expression goes. Most adults were irritated by him. His dad said he was a fidget and yelled at him even when other people were around.

The fidgety quality was what I liked in Pudge. He was always picking things up, examining them, and putting them down. Could be an acorn, could be a timepiece. It didn't bother me. He seemed receptive to life and to new things. I knew I could deliver these for him. Every time I took him to a natural cave, or a place hollowed out by blasting, or a spot where you could watch the river and no one could see you because the alders were thick, you could tell it was a whole new world for him. He had no siblings, and most other children avoided him. I loved to see him light up. You could see it in his eyes.

———

My first and favorite chore when the frost was on the ground was to take scoops of grain from the bin underneath the hayloft and carry them to the pullets and pheasants without spilling a seed. I loved the smell and texture of the grain bin. More than once I pushed my face into the grain, to get a

———

sandpaper bath from the sharp seeds. Once I buried myself in the grain in a game of "sardines," where one person is "it" and everyone else hides in a stationary location. I had been quickly found by Hannah.

"You can't hide from me, Jamieson Kooby," she said. "I know what you're going to do before you do, because I know what makes you tick and you don't."

"Sure," I had said. "Big deal." But I had been pleased by the attention.

"You want all the fun of being dead," said Hannah.

"Don't be ridiculous," I said as I climbed slowly from my snug place.

The air and the ground were dark on the Saturday after Thanksgiving as I carried two pewter scoops, tilted up to carry the maximum cargo without spilling, to the pheasant pen behind the barn. There was the beginning of a mist. The woods looked like gunmetal, while the earth was soft, giving in to every tread. I sucked in the air and rolled it on my tongue. Carpenter ants were at work on the staging at the end of the pheasants' pen. Normally I would have found it necessary to kill them, by force or fire. Today I smiled on them. They were obviously filled with purpose. Part of the system. Whose system? I thought. I decided it was my system, since I could banish the ants or not, as I chose.

I fed the pheasants and the pullets and the bantams and the regular chickens. I watched every grain, every bobbing head. What a piece of machinery! The birds settled down.

I was satisfied with the completion of the task and returned to the barn. My next chore was milking.

I settled myself on the stool without event, but when I

grasped Chloe's teat and began a rhythmic pumping, I became distracted. This was a production of nature that went well beyond me. The teat was warm, the milk was warm and cascading; between my legs I was instantly hard as a rock. This condition obtained while I milked all three cows. Francis Perrault happened by as I was concluding with Amaryllis, and elected to make small talk. I could not stand up, for obvious reasons. Francis could see I had no reason to linger on the stool, patting Amaryllis idiotically on her back. I wished him damnation for his lackadaisical whistle—obviously he was doing this to torment me. With a superior shrug he shambled off.

When I came back to the house I found Ettie Clark and Francis coming out the back door. Miss Ettie never used the back door, that was how she announced her status as a family member. She was crying. I had not seen her cry before, but I thought nothing of it.

After lunch I was sitting on top of Bald Hill with Hilliard Wood, Mehetable Hughes, and Ruth Ann Catlin, playing mumblety-peg with my jackknife. The girls had frocks on and were not careful with their knees, so I had a glimpse of the inside of a leg, above the knee.

There were dry oak leaves on the ground, curled up like scarabs, the sun shining through to the bright green underneath. The roof of my mouth felt dry. I wanted to say something for the benefit of the girls, but couldn't think what.

"Look!" said Hilliard, pointing up.

A red-tailed hawk was wheeling over us. I thought it was scouting rodents, but soon saw what Hilliard had seen: a crow was flying just behind the hawk's ear, pecking and shrieking.

"Why doesn't the redtail eat him?" asked Ruth Ann.

"The crow can maneuver better, he can always get higher than the hawk," said Hilliard.

"Ohh," said Ruth Ann, brushing her hair away from her face. She lay down on the leaves to stare at the sky, to stare at the hawk and the crow. Her arm touched Hilliard's leg. Her skirt had bunched up well above her knee. I waited for her to push it down but she didn't. She had freckles on the inside of her thigh.

On our return to the farm that afternoon, I volunteered to help Francis slaughter two of the pigs in the gated area next to the sty, behind the barn. It was high time for that anyway. Two years earlier a wild dog had got in and killed one of the largest pigs, and we lost the meat and the revenue. "No time like the present," I said to Francis as we picked up the rope and buckets and the axe from the shed. This was something I had heard Grandma say. I was not sure of its meaning, except that it was generally followed by action of some sort, and I was interested in a change of scene. We made short work of the pigs. Afterward I stood by the split-rail fence and turned the outdoor hose on my hands and forearms.

Miss Ettie called to me from her window that she had something for me. She had seen me washing off the blood at the faucet. I walked up the back stairs with nothing on but my trousers. There was still blood on my arm. I had never been in her room with her before, but I thought nothing of it. The roof of my mouth was dry and the stirring had returned. I was throbbing beneath my dungarees. Miss Ettie saw this and pressed her hand against the front of my trousers. "I'm wet too," she said. I said I didn't understand. She took my hand and guided it beneath her skirt—I thought nothing of this, either. She was right, she was wet. She undid the buckle on the front of my dungarees and pulled me over onto her sofa. We heard Francis walking in the yard by the barn. Miss Ettie clamped her hand over my mouth, hard. She removed it and replaced it with her mouth. Her tongue was warm. She was warm below too. I locked my arms around her back and poured myself into her. I was outside my own body, looking at us. "We're underwater," I whispered. The material of her dress must have been thin for the season, as her skin showed goose bumps wherever I touched. Something made me kiss the back of her head, underneath where her hair was gathered.

Miss Ettie pulled my head past her so I couldn't look at her.

"I try to be good, and I can't," she snuffled into my ear. "I get so I have to get my hands on a man."

My eyes popped open. I was a man.

Miss Ettie caressed the back of my head. "You have an eye for beauty, Jamieson," she said. "You must be sure to keep it."

Winter

GRANDMA baked a pheasant for lunch on the first Sunday in December. She made a sauce out of milk and bread and nutmeg, setting it on the stove for an hour with a full onion in the pot. She ground brown bread into crumbs and fried it with butter and salt. An open bowl of red currant jelly was set between me and Caleb. It never moved.

When the last plate was cleared—Grandma forbade stacking at the table—Caleb and I were out the door like shots, our slings in our back pockets. Hannah was leaning against an iron stile by the edge of the barn, chewing gum, as we tore downhill for the pond and its lush tenantry of birds and frogs. She stopped us in our tracks by proffering two sticks of gum between thumb and forefinger.

Hannah looked at me. "Where are you going?"

"Pond. Thanks."

"Come on along!" said Caleb. But Hannah didn't move. She was still looking at me. She must know, I thought. Maybe they all know, all women, just by looking.

I walked over to her, holding her eye, and straightened out her arm by the elbow, propelling her forward down the muddy path. She seemed satisfied with this and began to move on her own steam.

As we hit the edge of the wood it began to rain, without authority.

"I love rain," I said.

"Mmm," said Hannah.

"It deadens and quickens at the same time," I said.

Caleb looked at me.

"It deadens the forest floor, for noise, but it quickens the green and white that's peeking through," I said.

"Fascinating," said Caleb. The conversation was not going well.

I took Hannah's elbow in my hand again, but just held it, didn't straighten out her arm.

"I love it because it covers you," she said. "Not that no one can see you, just that no one will look. They'd get rain in their eyes. And it makes you move. A chilly drop gets you going." I felt vindicated.

A breeze swept the rain around in currents. I was pleased by the look of the alders whipped by the wind, bent down then springing up. Like Shaker women rejoicing in church, throwing up their hands.

I looked at Hannah's face. She was smiling. I looked at her

arm. I was still holding it. It was covered with goose bumps on account of the rain.

Caleb and I had a grackle and a starling to our credit along the hill, one shot from a cedar and one from a poplar. When we came to the pond, we turned our aim to the heavens for the sheer joy of it and let fly with our best stones, round pink ones, straight into the air. When Caleb finally fished in his pocket and found no more, he looked so regretful I wanted to laugh.

"Plenty more where those came from," I said.

———

DAVID Richards was the sheriff of the five towns. He had sandy hair, muscular arms, and the complexion of one who lived outdoors as much as he could. He was an exceptionally gentle man; I thought it odd that he made his living by locking people up. Sheriff Richards and his wife had had a son, Sammy, the same age as Caleb and I, who had been killed four years earlier in a squirrel hunting accident, another boy's rifle discharging into the back of his neck. The sheriff never said a word against the other boy or his parents. He still went hunting a good deal and took Caleb and me with him. He never spoke about his son. Neither did we, although we had known him. Quiet boy, with a round fuzzy head, hair always cropped close by Annie Richards, the sheriff's wife. Annie had loved to run her hand over the top of her son's head. Then she would hold him and sniff at the back of his neck. "Are you mine?" she would say. She was pretending she was on a scientific mission, instead of just

———

wanting to bury her face in the back of his neck. The first
time I understood that was in Miss Ettie's room.

Sheriff Richards had a hunting shack on high ground in
New Salem. We called it the Heart of Africa because it had a
stool made out of an elephant's foot. When you cranked up
the wood-burning stove it got to be about a hundred degrees
in a hurry, so it was easy to believe you were in Africa. Two
of the walls were covered with seines: big nets on poles, with
cork bobbers along the top edge and lead sinkers at the bottom. Four men could drain a small pond of bass with these
contraptions in half an hour. We used them when we wanted
to seed a newly dug pond with mature fish. The ponds in the
Valley held both smallmouth and largemouth, with a few
pickerel. The trout kept mainly to the moving water, like the
Swift and its feeders.

The sheriff owned two canvas hunting coats that looked as
though they dated from the previous century, and probably
did. They were cut short at the waist. Neither had ever been
washed, and the fabric was stiff with the dried blood of generations of animals and birds. He left these coats standing
straight up on the floor of the Heart of Africa, the right arm of
each crooked into a salute. After use they were returned to
the same position. So the redoubt was always manned.

On the third wall two stuffed squirrels, fox and cat, raced
after each other in perpetual lust. One horizontal beam held
boxes of ammunition and cleaning materials; another, two
mallard decoys and a pintail. The smell of Hoppe's gun oil
dominated the room during season.

The land around this camp became part of what they call
the buffer zone for the reservoir, taken but not submerged. So

you can still tramp it. Most years I go back in December or January. There's nothing inside the shack, and the stovepipe has been unhooked. I like to go in and open a bottle of Hoppe's to get the old smells going. That makes it seem warmer.

For deer hunting, Sheriff Richards used an old flintlock, a beautiful silver-inlay piece. He said it made him feel more of a tie to the hunters of generations gone by. "The deer still look and act the same as a hundred years ago," he said. "There's no reason we shouldn't."

The Richardses were old-fashioned. They had a painting of Saint Hubert over their bed, staring in wonder at the stag and the white cross burning in the night. It was and still is my favorite work of art.

The sheriff was the only hunter in the Valley still holding to the flintlock. He handled it with reverence. He handled everything with reverence when he had us with him on a hunting trip. "The outdoors is my cathedral," he would say.

——————

In all the times I hunted with him, I never saw Sheriff Richards kill a doe, though it was lawful to do so and they were far more plentiful than bucks. That was before you needed a permit to shoot a doe.

Two days before Christmas 1937, several inches of powder had fallen when the sheriff led me and Caleb to try our luck at New Salem. From a distance the hills looked unshaven, the hardwoods like dirty whiskers against the snow on the ground.

——————

It was rough hunting terrain, up and down, lots of criss-crossed fallen trees. The scene was softened by the snow: every blowdown had its own thatched roof of white, hanging over the edges like a fungus. The felled trees were candy canes covered with glistening sugar icing. There was bright sun. Worst possible hunting conditions. Until I moved my left hand up the barrel and touched cold steel, I had forgotten why we had come. The chill made me alert again. I thought of what Hannah had said about rain.

My eyes swept the terrain of evergreen, rock, and ice, looking for something out of place. Anything out of place—a darker or softer shape, any horizontal line, any movement—could be game or could lead to game. Horizontals are unusual in nature, except for an animal's back.

As we crested a hill, the unreality of the scene continued. Dead trees creaked overhead in the breeze. An icy boulder was covered with moss of an incongruous green. A beautiful doe stood athwart our path, staring straight at us, looking for all the world like a Christmas tree ornament. She could not have failed to hear us. She blinked once, twice.

"Shoot!" said Caleb from behind us.

"Right," said the sheriff. I saw him raise his rifle in slow motion, aim it with his customary smooth swing straight at the deer's shoulder, then pull it to the side with a jerk and fire, missing the deer by three feet. She was gone in an instant, behind a stand of pines.

"Darn!" said the sheriff. Caleb ran up to us.

"Wasn't it a clear shot?" he asked.

"Just missed, is all," said the sheriff. "Not my day."

Caleb seemed puzzled. I wasn't, but I kept my mouth shut.

———

B I L L Crocker was the only doctor in the five towns. He lived at the end of Brush Lane in Ripton, at the foot of Basking Ridge, pretty much all by himself, him and the possums and porcupines. He was in his early forties but had grown older than his years, owing perhaps to hurrying from place to place to keep up with life and death in the Valley. His dark hair was streaked with white both in front and at the temples. He brushed it straight back. His eyes were unusually large, as though on the watch for disaster. He smoked constantly, Old Golds and Pall Malls.

Doc Crocker lived on the place he was born in. His parents had died in a barn fire, trying to save their horses. She went in for him when he didn't come right out. Young Billy had been over at the Bennetts' in Belchertown when it happened. He said he wished he had been home. I bet he did.

He boarded up their house and went away to a college in New York soon after, then south to Louisiana for medical studies at Tulane University. Grandma said no one in the Valley figured to see him again, but he kept in touch by letter with the Bennett family. He was a general practitioner in New Orleans. Then the letters stopped, and one day he was on the train platform at Orange. Nobody met him, as he hadn't said he was coming, but he found his way to his old homestead all right and seemed to enjoy settling in. There was no mortgage on the place, never had been. Grandma took me and Caleb over to help him get the boards off the windows and give the house a coat of paint.

———

"Right neighborly of you," Doc Crocker had said to Grandma.

"On the contrary, this is selfish of s," she had said. "Everyone loves seeing a house come back." Doc Crocker smiled and stared at the ground, still holding a claw hammer and a chisel, but not moving on to the work.

No one was sure why Bill Crocker returned to the Valley, after all he had seen. Some said it was to marry the Bennett girl. She had had a shock from a broken engagement while he was down in Louisiana, and her system was not the same as before. Doc Crocker never did marry the girl, but did visit her three or four times a year, bringing her things. I don't think her case of nerves made the least never-mind to him. I think he saw right through it to the girl she had been, and that was all there was to it. He had caught a glimpse of her in a certain pose once, and that's what stayed with him. That's what I think anyway. We didn't find out, because in the mid-thirties her nerves broke completely and she was put in the institution in Belchertown, where she died a year later.

Folks said that Doc Crocker spent rather too much time at Conkey's Tavern. It was true he could be found there three or four evenings a week. No one saw him with an unsteady hand, though, morning or night. Uncle Ed said he had developed a depression while in New Orleans, said people were given to strange elixirs and compounds in that part of the country. Grandma said he deserved a drink after bearing witness to suffering all day long.

Doc Crocker didn't sit off to the side by himself when he went to the tavern—it was more or less impossible to do so—but he didn't mix it up much either. He would listen and was not hesitant to give his opinion on matters of medicine, but didn't offer much more, certainly nothing of a personal nature. As drunk as men might get at Conkey's, no one ever mentioned the name of the Bennett girl. The only time anyone saw the color rise in Doc Crocker's cheek was when Red Barnes had had a deal too much whiskey and made everyone in the establishment be quiet so he could ask the doctor "an important *medical* question." Folks obliged, mainly to get Red to shut up. Red hooked his thumbs behind his suspenders and stumbled over until his face was too close to Doc Crocker's. Doc was looking into his own shot glass, which was full. He stubbed out his cigarette.

"Now here," said Red, "is my important medical question. My important medical question is, why were you fool enough to come back to the Valley?" He turned around smiling, expecting guffaws. No one moved a muscle.

"You could have stayed on Cayuga, you could have taken up residence among the fleshpots of the French. Why on earth—"

No one saw Doc Crocker get up, but there he was on his feet, his drink in his hand, nose to nose with Red, who quieted down.

"I'll tell you why, Red," said Doc Crocker. He turned to the side, drained his glass, set it down, and turned back to Red. He breathed into Red's face.

"Because I had my reasons."

Doc Crocker walked out the door without paying, which was not his way. Thomas Trimble, the proprietor, said he had no expression on his face on the way out. He stayed away for the next three nights and paid when he came back.

———

———

CHRISTMAS Day was fine and cold. A sparkling dust, fallen during the night, touched up the earth's lovely face.

I walked straight out the front door at seven o'clock. Earth and sky were well lit; I felt the atmosphere was embracing me. I returned the favor, my arms spread wide, inviting the air to knife into my flannels.

Grandma had promised me a major gift for Christmas morning, having skipped my birthday present in October to permit its purchase.

I looked at the snow blowing off the pines down the hill directly in front of our house. I thought that if there is a God, he is in his heaven. At the same time I thought that if there is not a God, this brightness is all the more for me.

I must have felt guilty about this last thought, because I jumped at the voice of Uncle Ed behind me.

"Merry Christmas, young feller. Are you sure you don't want an overcoat?"

I turned and shook his hand, forcing myself to smile. Uncle Ed looked the part of town clerk: well-trimmed pepper-and-salt hair, rimless spectacles, a squinting, quizzical expression above a thin mustache, mouth usually drawn down, cleft chin. He kept himself in good physical shape by walking over a dozen miles every day, and he was Grandma's only living link to the man she had loved. I would have given as much to have known Bill Hardiman as I would to have known my own father or mother longer. I never tired of

———

Grandma telling me how Bill Hardiman would clap a shy person on the back or light up a dull room of people by walking in the door, or keep quiet when he could easily have said a smart thing.

I was wondering what Bill Hardiman's imperfections might have been when I realized Uncle Ed was talking to me.

"Jamieson! Where is your head, lad?"

"Sorry."

"That's all right. I was asking whether the fire is all set for the meal."

"I was on my way out to do that."

"Very good. I'll be in to wish your grandmother a merry Christmas. Here," he said, flipping me his cigarette lighter. I caught it. It had a bolt of lightning on the side. Uncle Ed tipped an imaginary hat in my direction.

I walked around to the field of buckwheat behind the house, where the deer often stood three or four thick in the morning. There were none there today. I supposed that they were home celebrating Christmas with their families.

Toward the far edge of the field we had dug a pit four feet deep. By its edge were smooth rocks selected from bygone walls on the property.

After a few minutes of gathering small sticks and breaking larger ones over my knee, I lined the base of the pit with kindling. In the center I created a tepee of smaller sticks, housing enough air so that Uncle Ed's lighter set the whole floor of the pit to blazing.

Backing out just before the flames reached my feet, I picked my way to a stand of fallen birches in search of larger logs. I must not have been in this particular spot for a year, for I soon came upon a well-preserved stump lying entirely above ground. I would never have let that treasure pass if I had seen it before.

For a child bent on fire, there is nothing like a stump. The gods of the underground pack every sizzling juice they can think of into every stump that has been dead a year or more but not yet rotted. I rolled my prize into the clearing, thinking how the flames would shoot into the air. I threw on another layer of brush, mostly alders plus some heavy viburnum, to keep the fire going until the guests arrived. My chore over and my sense of purpose satisfied, I noticed the cold biting at my ankles and trotted back to the house.

Grandma and Uncle Ed were drinking coffee in the front room, admiring our Christmas tree. I had cut it myself from Thayer's Wood, just over the Enfield-Ripton line. It was a six-foot spruce, well proportioned, and decorated with a few flannel ornaments that had been in Grandma's family for generations.

Uncle Ed set down his mug. "To work, to work, good men of the village," he said in a merry way. "Time for presents!" Grandma nodded and smiled.

Grandma and Uncle Ed exchanged slim volumes of the philosopher Nietzsche, which was a well-worn joke between them. Grandma was as close to an intellectual, or a bluestocking, as you were likely to find in the Swift River Valley. She was from upstate New York, a first cousin of one of the leading suffragettes at Seneca Falls. Her family had thought her bound for college, but she lost her heart to Bill Hardiman

while he was making a sales swing through Onondaga and
Seneca Counties on behalf of a farm equipment manufac-
turer. When he came back the next spring, she went back to
Massachusetts with him and never returned. Uncle Ed used
to remark ruefully that she "outfarmed the farmers" in the
Valley, but the truth is she was raised on a farm in the Finger
Lakes district and, despite her considerable library, had both
feet firmly planted in the dirt.

Uncle Ed, for his part, had no more idea than I did what
the contents of his Nietzsche volume could possibly mean.
He and Grandma gave each other the same volumes each
year, back and forth.

"Oh! *Thus Spake Zarathustra!*" he said in mock delight.
"My favorite!" This pleased Grandma, and therefore pleased
me as well.

I gave Uncle Ed a cigar and he gave me a whetstone. Fair
enough.

To Grandma, knowing that this would be our last
Christmas in the Valley, I gave a bobwhite quail carved in
wood, on which I had labored in the attic much of the fall.
She knew what it meant to me and why I was giving it to her,
and after giving me a brief kiss on the forehead when she saw
what it was, had to leave the room for a minute. I have been
here before, I thought.

For my part, I received a secondhand but serviceable Daisy
air rifle. I was thrilled.

"It's from Uncle Ed, too," said Grandma weakly as I was
caressing the stock of the gun.

"Don't point that thing in the room," said Uncle Ed. "If

you are going to move it around, make sure you are outdoors or it's pointed at the ceiling."

"It's got to be pointed somewhere, Uncle Ed," I said. "As long as it isn't pointed at another person, what's the difference?"

"Now, now," said Grandma. "Maybe you should go see if it works on those nasty grackles you feel so threatened by." Grandma and I had a bargain that I could kill grackles and starlings to my heart's delight, provided I would not trouble her precious songbirds. I did not consider blue jays to be a songbird, and never asked Grandma her view on the matter.

When we were done with the presents, Grandma put the beans and cabbage on. I went out for a walk down the lane and shot a cowbird off the fence. A blue jay called me a thief and I killed him too. I went over to the pit and laid a layer of rocks on, then the meat and potatoes right on the stones.

A little before noon Doc Crocker came over on horseback from Basking Ridge, and David and Annie Richards turned up in a buckboard. They all exchanged small decorative presents with Grandma and Uncle Ed—oranges with cloves, bricks covered in cloth to make a doorstop, and the like. They sat in the front room with the windows open to help them enjoy a glass of "shooting sherry," which Doc Crocker had bought in Petersham. He passed around a fresh pack of Old Golds, and everybody was takers.

We brought the plates with the beans and cabbage outdoors, and sat at the picnic table a few feet from the pit. I removed the meat and potatoes. We had our own butter, too. I had my first glass of sherry and it made me dizzy. I almost stumbled into the pit when I was going back over to roll in the big stump. I pretended it was all an act, but I caught Grandma's eye and decided not to have any more sherry. The stump did go up like a rocket, and I got compliments for that.

Caleb came over after lunch and we went down to the little pond, cleared off some snow, and played at ice hockey with sticks from a fallen beech and a perfectly round wooden puck that had to have been sawed from a fence post. We fought to a tie, three goals to three.

The grown-ups cut holes in the ice at the other end of the pond, where it was no more than a few feet deep, and dropped hand lines down. A number of small yellow perch were caught in this fashion. Annie Richards screamed for her husband. It was a happy scream, not worrisome. The sheriff helped her drag in the biggest pickerel I ever saw come out of that pond, twenty-six inches and three and a half pounds. Doc Crocker, who had been pulling on the sherry bottle in the finest ice-fishing tradition, unfolded a long knife from his pocket and filleted the fish right on the ice with two motions: down behind the head, then back down along the rib cage to the tail. He peeled the skin off the other side of the fillet without even using the knife. My hands would have been too cold for that.

At four o'clock Sheriff Richards invited Caleb and me to go with him to jump the Rye Pond and the Teal Hole. Grandma said I might use Grandpa Bill Hardiman's Parker twenty-gauge, as it was a special occasion. She never took it back from me and I keep that gun on the wall of my bedroom to this day. It has a strip of orange rubber at the base of the stock, so it must have been too short for him when he got it. I never look at that gun without thinking of Bill Hardiman, whom I never met.

The suspense involved in sneaking up on a pond to surprise ducks on the water, particularly late in the afternoon, is considerable. Usually you have no idea what awaits you, but you must exercise care not to make a sound. Generally the ducks are bunched in the few unfrozen areas.

The approach to the Teal Hole was single file along a ditch bordered on both sides by heavy brambles. Sheriff Richards went first because of the brambles, holding his gun over his head to avoid scratching it. I did the same with the Parker twenty. After a hundred yards we took a right turn down a narrower but deeper ditch. The footing was difficult because of fallen limbs and because you had to keep your left foot on one side of the ditch and your right foot on the other. The brambles made passage otherwise impossible.

Twenty yards from the pond we heard the low contented muttering of black ducks at their feed, then a higher-pitched quack of alarm, then a whoosh of water and no further quacking. We froze. I heard a whistle directly over my head but dared not look up. After a moment the sheriff turned around.

"Widgeon," he said. "Three widgeon and two black duck way on the other edge of the pond. We would not have had a shot anyway. Let's try the Rye Pond."

We left as we had come, then tramped overland all the way past Sunk Pond, grateful for the chance to stretch our legs. My right foot was damp, having slipped into the ditch. The cold did not bother me but the squelching sound made by the water in my shoe would have been fatal to our mission, so I stopped to wring out my sock, breaking my gun as a safety measure. While I was standing on one leg a pintail single flew right over my head. Caleb pointed, but no one said a word. Not worth a shot.

The approach to the Rye Pond was the opposite of that required for the Teal Hole. The pond had been created by a dragline shovel in the middle of a large field; it was surrounded by flatland and was built up three or four feet at its edge. Cattails and phragmites grew on this raised land, so the birds in the pond could not see you coming. They were quite likely to hear you if you tried to sneak up on them, though, so we would run straight at them the last fifty yards, hoping to crest the hill while they were still confused.

The wind was in our favor, and to my amazement the ducks were still swimming in circles as we came up over the hill. "Whoosh!" shouted the sheriff. The ducks took off in all directions.

Like many inexperienced hunters, I had difficulty selecting my target, first following and then abandoning a group of black ducks and mallards that were almost out of my range when they got up. I turned to my right to find a teal, who had been hiding close to the bank, just taking off. I covered him with the Parker, released the safety, and saw him thrust down into the water. I turned to my left and saw one black duck dead in the water and another swimming away. Another shot from the sheriff created a pattern in the water around his head, and he too rolled over.

"I didn't mean to hit him, but he went down on the first

shot," said the sheriff. "If I hadn't finished him off, the foxes would have him by supper time."

Back at the house Doc Crocker debreasted the black ducks and the teal. The sheriff told the others of his curious double, and Grandma cooked up all of nature's bounty, fish and fowl, in the skillet, adding only butter and vinegar.

My last Christmas in the Swift River Valley was my best.

———

SOMEBODY was abroad who shouldn't have been during the week between Christmas and New Year's, because the Valley had three barn fires in four days. The first two were not much more than outbuildings: a crib and silo on Amisted Ames's in Greenwich, and a shed and some stalls, fortunately not in use, on the Wheeler farm in Enfield. Then two nights before New Year's Eve the big barn on the Twynham place in Prescott went up like a torch. Hannah came by to tell us at breakfast time.

Uncle Ed was fiddling with his spoon. "How did you know about this, Hannah?" he asked. Grandma gave him a look.

"How did I know about it? You could hear the horses screaming all the way from the poor farm, before you could see anything. Woke us all up. The Twynhams' man got them out just in time, but that was about all he could do. It lit up the sky all over Prescott."

"Must have been pretty exciting," said Uncle Ed.

"It was," said Hannah.

"Did you go over?" said Uncle Ed.

———

"We all did."

"You and Jimmy Toolbox and Honus Hasby?"

"Jimmy Toolbox and I and the women. Honus was visiting a friend somewhere else."

"So no one was looking after things."

"I wouldn't say that."

"Did you all go over together?"

"Yes, we all went over together, but there was nothing to be done."

"People say there are ghosts in Prescott," said Uncle Ed. "Maybe the ghosts set the fire. Did you see any ghosts there, Hannah?"

"No, Mr. Hardiman. Not last night."

"Three barn fires in four nights is quite a coincidence," said Uncle Ed.

"Maybe it's some of the folks from Boston, trying to save themselves a little work," said Grandma.

I was glad when breakfast was over. Hannah led me on a walk down the lane. The morning was fresh.

"I'll tell you what, though," she said.

"What?"

"Let's give the ashes a day or two to cool down, and it will be worth our while to go through that rubble. I remember liking to be in that barn. There's something special there, something valuable."

"Did you hide it there when you were Oriel?"

"I don't think I hid it, I think I found it, when I was young, three or four."

"Let's go New Year's Day early." My thought was to lessen the risk of interference from grown-ups, especially the volunteer firefighters who had nothing better to do than return to a fire scene day after day, to reassert their authority.

———

J U S T after sunup I tiptoed down to the kitchen, wedged two of Grandma's sugar cookies into my mouth, and made for the trail through the woods that brings you out a half mile from the poor farm in Prescott. My walk was an ecstatic experience: I allowed the cookies to dissolve, rather than chewing them, so my taste buds were bathed in pleasure for the duration. I swallowed the last bit only when I saw Hannah waiting at the end of the trail, her hands on her hips.

"Whatchew been eating?" she said as I drew up.

Instinctively I swallowed again to make sure there would be no visible evidence. "What do you mean?" I said.

"You've been eating something good. Never mind, I'm not hungry, let's go."

"Have you had breakfast?"

"Breakfast? At the poor farm? Yes, I cooked myself a couple of omelets made out of pheasant eggs, had a few of those sausages that you have to go to Worcester to get, and washed the whole thing down with champagne. It's New Year's Day, after all."

"That's what I figured." Why had I not had the wit to bring a cookie for Hannah?

She read my mind. "It's okay, come on, let's go." She squeezed my arm with both hands and we made good time to the Twynham place.

There's no chimney in a barn, so nothing was standing.

———

The two big wagons had left nothing behind but their wheels. Generations of steel farm equipment that had hung in proud ranks on the wall lay in scattered heaps. My first instinct was to pick up the blades: Jed, the Twynhams' man, would never have let them touch the ground, much less lie there. But there was nowhere to put them.

"Get your exploring head on," said Hannah. "We'll have to sift through the stuff. Pretend you're hunting, except the game is underground. Look for something that doesn't fit."

This was good advice, and in fact it was I who first spied the crack in the burned flooring that led us to the trapdoor.

"This was the little room with the stove," said Hannah. "I used to hide here in winter because it was nice and warm."

We pried open the trapdoor with a length of iron railing still warm to the touch.

"From the sliding door," said Hannah. "This was part of the bottom railing."

"You're just showing off," I said.

"Something was hidden near where it was comfy."

Under the trapdoor was a space two feet on either side, containing the ashes of some finery, and a black tin box.

"I remember silks or lace being in here," said Hannah. "They were my mother's. The box is after my time."

"Not anymore," I said, lifting the box out and setting it respectfully down. There was a lock on the front, but the hasp had broken off from the top, so I was able to lift the lid with my bare hands.

Inside were more ashes, and three silver dollars. Gorgeous ladies, proud eagles. I inspected each of them.

"Eighteen ninety-eight, every one," I said.

"Well after my time, as I thought," said Hannah.

We each took a dollar, and I took one for Caleb. "I'll go over to his place and give it to him right now," I said, remembering the cookies.

"You know what we have to do?" said Hannah.

"What?"

"We have to come back to this spot ten years from this minute, on New Year's in nineteen forty-eight. That will be the fiftieth anniversary of when these were minted. We can all show our dollars, Caleb too, to prove we know how to save something."

There was something troubling to me in this plan. "Or you and I could keep ours in the same place, to make sure we don't lose them, and we can just come together and meet Caleb here," I said.

"That sounds okay."

I did deliver Caleb's silver dollar to him that afternoon. He said we should all go and hide the three dollars together, which we did, in a cave near the top of Mount Zion. But on New Year's Day 1948, I was the only one of the three of us who came.

———

IN the winter the snow made the Valley a huge mixing bowl. A common motif was red on white, blood on the snow, either from coon hunting behind blueticks and black-and-tans or from animals going after one another in the barnyard. Sometimes even a bloody nose from a toboggan spill. The

———

Valley was ringed by outstanding toboggan country: Zion, Pomeroy, Lizzie, Russ, and the lesser hills.

We had a mess of skinny barn cats on our farm, gathering round at any sign of motion. They knew motion could mean food. Francis Perrault from somewhere got hold of a newfangled catch-'em-alive trap with two sections and a door between them that swung only one way. Caleb and I used it to catch brown rats, of which we had plenty. When we had four in the trap we invited Pudge Mullally over. Caleb told Mrs. Mullally we were going to play hide-and-seek in the barn. We set the trap on the snow between the barn and the corn crib. This drew several of the cats. Caleb and I held the cats, and Pudge got to spring the door of the trap. He was thrilled with the honor of it all. We gave the rats a twenty-foot head start—they came out blinking and sniffing, into the big cold open space, nothing like their stalls or hayloft—and then released the cats.

You know how a cat will worry a mouse, play with it? The barn cats didn't worry those rats a bit. They caught them in no time and killed them violently, first at the throat, then tearing the head from the body, then splitting the belly. There was blood on the snow, but not much, as those rats went down the gullet fast, fur and all. And some people are scared of rats! We never moved a muscle. Needless to say Pudge's eyes were like saucers.

"Can we do this again?" he asked.

"Sure, Pudge. Next time you can hold a cat if you like."

"I can hold a cat?"

"Sure," I said.

"I don't mind," said Pudge.

Soon after that, a big old barn tabby produced a litter of seven. Grandma said every cat in the barn would starve to death unless those kittens disappeared. She made me put them into a burlap bag, tie it, and slide it under the ice in French King Brook. The tabby was so swollen she could barely roll over when I was picking up the kittens, one by one. She had green eyes that didn't blink, just stabbed me. I never wanted to pick up a cat again.

As I look back on it, the cardinal points of my winter world were smoke, wind, ice, and blood.

———

F O R some of the older folks in the Valley, there were two more cardinal points: rum and whiskey. Once I had heard the story about Doc Crocker and Red Barnes, I longed to sit with the men at Conkey's Tavern. I had never had a drink of liquor but the one sherry at Christmas, but I wanted to see the men in their element.

Hannah told me I should definitely go, the later in the evening the better. "You learn more when you see people at their worst," she said. "If they are in an unfamiliar situation, they'll get edgy and say and do silly things you can learn from. Wrong things. Same when men have drink. Wrong things are more interesting."

One night in the middle of January I walked the three miles into town as soon as I had finished my chores at the farm. It was two hours past dark when I slipped into the back

———

of the big room at Conkey's. There were six tables but most everybody was standing, either in the middle of the room or at the big brass rail at the bar. A few of the younger men were interested in their reflections in the plate glass mirror behind the bar. The older ones stuck to their liquor and tobacco. There was a spittoon every six feet. The candles were down and flickering.

Trimble, the proprietor, was a small nervous fellow who resembled a muskrat. He led the way over to a dark corner and sat me down on a bench. "You can stay here, in Captain Shays's nook, but pipe down," he said. "There's been a good deal of politics today, and the spirits are higher than the flagons."

Through the smoke I could see Lawyer Kincaid, Sheriff Richards, and Doc Crocker in animated conversation with two of the local farmers, Putnam and Hodge. Preacher Moncrieff was leaning back against the bar, his elbows on the rail, taking it in.

"There is no way they can evict every person in the Valley," said Sheriff Richards, "if we stand together for our rights."

"There most certainly is," said Lawyer Kincaid. "All the legislature has to do is say so. Then it's the law. You are sworn to uphold the law, are you not?"

"The legislature should not forget the service of Captain Shays and the men of this Valley who fought at Breed's Hill and Lexington," said Sheriff Richards.

"Maybe they should and maybe they shouldn't," said Lawyer Kincaid. "That's not the point. The point is whether they will, not whether they should, and if not, then what? We are confronted not with a theory, but a condition. If we have a disciplined mind about this matter, we have to acknowledge that the important job is to make sure each property owner receives adequate compensation for the inevitable. That is my job, and that is what I am working for in Boston."

"What about my farm?" asked Wilbur Hodge, an enormous man in rough clothes. "You work your whole life, you lose it all? There's no compensation for that. There can't be."

Lawyer Kincaid put his hand on the man's shoulder. "You're a good man, Wilbur, but that's oversimplifying it," he said. "You're putting the horse before the cart."

"You're supposed to put the horse before the cart," said Doc Crocker. Lawyer Kincaid smiled and shook his head. Hodge looked doubtful, as though Lawyer Kincaid had the better of it.

"You build up a network," said Hodge. "How are they going to replace the network?"

"I'll tell you what," said Clayton Hawley, who was a selectman in Ripton. "If the legislature is going to give us money for our land, that's a sight better than what happened a hundred and fifty years ago. The merchants would give credit to people like me during poor harvests and then the banks would foreclose on us, without *any* compensation."

"That's exactly right," said Lawyer Kincaid.

The big man would have none of this. "I hope those wise students of the law in Boston will choke on their first taste of Swift River water." He took a gulp of his drink.

"No one will listen," said Lawyer Kincaid. "I am doing the

best I can." I noticed that Kincaid did not have a glass in his hand.

"You know, what we need is a newspaper," said Doc Crocker. "In politics, an event not covered by a newspaper is like a tree blowing down in a forest. Nobody pays any attention."

"It's the price of progress," said Lawyer Kincaid.

"It's the price of poor planning," said Sheriff Richards.

"The legislature has to consider matters from the point of view of all the people, not just a few," said Lawyer Kincaid.

"That's what they always say," said Doc Crocker. "In fact, the state sees only its needs, whether it is the railroad, or tax money, or water for the fine ladies and gentlemen. What about the farmers who have worked this land since the time of Shays? What about their needs? We marched east and saved their lives in seventeen seventy-six, they marched west and shot down Shays's men like rats in seventeen eighty-seven. Now here they are again." At this, the doctor succumbed to a fit of coughing. He set his glass on the bar to avoid spilling it.

There was a commotion at the door and Trimble stepped quickly over. Moncrieff was roused to action and sprang away from the bar.

"Don't let him in here," he commanded. "He is a vagrant."

Doc Crocker walked over to the door. "Have you got any money, Hammy?" he said.

"Of course not," said Hammy. "I just thought I would step in and listen to the learned folks, being as this is a free country."

———

"No one can come in here but regular patrons," said Preacher Moncrieff. "You have no business here."

Doc Crocker guided Hammy to the bar. "That's all right," he said, "I'll stand you a drink. Two whiskey," he said to Trimble, and dropped two coins on the bar.

A man seated on the barrel in the corner near me drew his pipe from his mouth and joined in.

"You oughtn't to touch that stuff, Doc, you know you really oughtn't."

"You're a fine one to talk, Asa. You had a few drinks, went out for deer, saw Mrs. Hatcher's harlequin Great Dane in the woods, and gave up hunting as well as drinking. Near as I can tell, you've given up going into the woods too, you just sit on that barrel smoking your pipe. I don't know as I need to profit by your example."

Asa shook his head. "Doc, you don't know the words you are saying."

"Are you impugning my sobriety?" said Doc Crocker.

"Easy, Doc, he's just joking," said Sheriff Richards, taking his elbow.

"No, he ain't," said Doc Crocker. He set down his glass. "But that's all right." He waved to Asa to show he wasn't sore.

Preacher Moncrieff said, "Doctor, you had no call to bring that vagrant in."

"What business is it of yours, exactly?" said Doc Crocker.

Lawyer Kincaid stepped between them. "It's everybody's business," he said. "We are trying to run decent towns around here, towns our children can be proud of. This man is a baleful influence, an example of what can happen when a person makes no demands upon himself."

This was too much for Sheriff Richards. "*You're* trying to run decent towns? You want to put our towns underwater! Talk about making demands on yourself!"

"Calm yourself," said Preacher Moncrieff. "It is not for us to challenge the unfathomable workings of providence."

The next morning I asked Grandma what this meant. She shook her head. I must have looked puzzled. She touched my shoulder.

"I suppose what it means, Jamieson, is that not everybody has the same cathedral, even those that have the same church."

―――

Not everybody had the same church, for that matter. A few days later I was over to Uncle Ed's little white clapboard house, with the nice red maples in front and the trellis and the grapevines out back. I was poking around in the potting shed and came on a stack of old flyers announcing work opportunities for the Central Mass. Railroad, old Gebetti's line that never got finished. After touting the glamour and the high pay for a time, the leaflet stated in boldface: WORK CREW TO BE 100% PROTESTANT; NO LABOR STOPPAGE OR UNREST EXPECTED OR TOLERATED.

I brought the stack into the house, where Uncle Ed was smoking his pipe in the living room, reading the latest newspaper from Worcester and frowning. He brightened when he saw the flyers.

"I had forgotten about those," he said, setting down his pipe and taking the flyers in both hands. He examined them

―――

as a mother might a newborn. "Honeycutt printed these up for us at no charge, given the gravity of the issue," he said. "Say what you will about that ladies' man Signore Gebetti, he knew how to go about a thing in the right way."

Uncle Ed explained that many recent arrivals to Boston from the cities of Europe had a religion called Catholics, and part of their religion was they were not to work for more than a few weeks without beginning to complain about the conditions, ask for time off, and generally sabotage whatever enterprise they had been engaged on.

I asked if they had sabotaged the construction of the Central Mass. Railroad.

"No, those leaflets did the trick," said Uncle Ed, tapping them onto his table for emphasis. "If Signore Gebetti hadn't had more pressing business at home, that road would stretch halfway to Ohio by now."

"Are there any Catholics in the Valley?"

"You know Irishtown, off Greenwich Center?"

"Yep."

"Everybody in Irishtown is Catholics. Also Patrick Mullally and his missus. And it wouldn't surprise me if your friend Hammy wasn't Catholics too."

"Hammy is an Indian. He's a Wampanoag."

"He could be both. Could have been both."

"Is Pudge Mullally Catholics?"

"Sure. If his parents are Catholics, he's a Catholics."

"I never heard them talk about it."

"They don't live in Irishtown, so they don't go to that little hall they use for a church. Could be, in fairness, Pudge doesn't know he's Catholics."

"What do Catholics do?"

"The women are all right, they're hard workers, but the men drink whiskey till they lie around, and they vote Democrat."

"What's a Democrat?"

"Never mind. I'll tell you what explains it, Jamieson. You remember last spring there was a commotion about goblins abroad in Prescott and Greenwich?"

"I do." I knew Hannah had had a good deal of trouble over this at the poor farm. She had even advised me against being a goblin at Halloween.

"Well, a lot of that was put out by old Buzzy Phelps and the Lithcott lad, to stir up the folks in Irishtown. What with all their saints and statues, they're terrible afraid of spirits. On Saturday night Buzzy and young Lithcott raced down the street in Irishtown, saying to all they met that the goblins had been cornered in Parson's Hollow, that a couple of farmers had them pinned up against those big oaks and they couldn't get out."

"I never heard about that."

"Indeed you didn't. Nobody in Irishtown wanted to tell about that! Seems every man in Irishtown that could lay his hands on a firearm was off to Parson's Hollow, half of them with a jug on the other arm, and when they got there, lo and behold, there's two flickering lights right up against the old oaks, just as they'd been told. They didn't dare approach too close, of course, so they took cover behind pines fifty yards off, and popped away at those lights till mostly morning. A great cheer went up when one of the lights went out after a hundred rounds or so, but they never did get the other. Then when it got light they went over and saw it was nothing but a pair of old rubber boots with holes cut in the side and candles stuck in the heel. No, there were very few reports issuing from Irishtown about that evening's activities."

———

I asked Hannah about the haunted boots in Irishtown. She said she had heard all about it at the time from Honus Hasby, who couldn't stop laughing over it.

"I feel bad for them they don't have a real church," she said. "Particularly since so many Valley folks who have fine white wooden churches don't seem to enjoy them."

"What do you mean?"

"Let's go to the church in Ripton, Saturday when it's quiet, and I'll show you around."

"You can't show me anything I don't know, that's one of our churches."

She laid a finger against her lips.

As soon as my chores were done on Saturday morning I slipped down the lane with my air rifle, stowed it in a hollow hickory, and doubled back below the cornfields to meet Hannah on the road. She was waiting, as usual.

We didn't see a soul as we neared the church in Ripton, but that didn't make me feel any easier about the business.

"Are we going to march in the front door? I don't think it works except on Sundays. And what'll we say if someone sees us, or if someone's inside?"

She took my arm and guided me down to the back of the building, against the hill, where the ground was lower.

———

"What's back here? I've never been here."

She pointed to the basement wall.

"What?"

She stepped over and pushed open a large door on rails. "You don't see anything if you don't have your eyes open," she said.

"You mean praying?"

"I mean always going in the front door."

We stepped into the church basement. The only light came from the doorway. We moved away from it so our eyes could adjust. There were chairs, tables, candles, books. "So?" I said.

Hannah took a candle and lit it. She slid out a board in the wall, at eye level. I saw folded white robes, which had never in my experience been used in services on the floor above. Something brass lay on top.

"What's that?"

"A censer. This is a chalice. This is a pentacle."

"What are they for? This is like another treasure chest, without a trapdoor."

"Right. Try this." She withdrew another object from the wall space and put it in my hand. My fingers closed on it. It was a dagger.

"Hold this too." She put a stick of some sort in my other hand.

"You're a natural," she said.

We heard a tread overhead. Hannah took the objects from me and restored them to their hiding place, sliding the panel shut.

"What do we say if we're caught?" My heart was thumping.

"Just say we're worshiping. That's what everybody else does."

———

The tread overhead went away, so we didn't get a chance to try out our story.

———

ON February 1, the Water Supply Commission sent every farmer in the Valley a legal notice ordering them to leave their property by September 1. It said compensation could be withheld if arrangements had not been finalized in a timely fashion. All public buildings in all five towns were to be put up for auction on June 10, with their contents, and the winning bidders would have until August 1 to remove their property, or all would be demolished.

These letters were the dominant topic of church services that Sunday. Grandma took me and Doc Crocker to Ripton, where there was a considerable hum among the congregants in the hall. I saw Pudge and his mother, so I guessed maybe they weren't Catholics after all. David Richards and the other vestrymen stood at the back, handing out flyers for that day's exercises. Grandma touched him on the elbow, nodding slightly to the side. He escorted us to a side pew. I like the side pews better because you can look either at the preacher or into the crowd. You can see people's faces when they think no one's looking at them.

"What do you suppose our leaders will make of the notices to quit?" Grandma whispered. "Now the hammer has dropped, I can't wait to see how they'll explain it all away."

"Charles will think of something," said Doc Crocker. His jaw set as the dark robe of Preacher Moncrieff swirled past. The man seemed a walking shadow.

———

"He looks to have had a hard night," Grandma whispered.

"Every night is hard when you are God's chosen instrument and there is so much evil abroad in the land," said the doctor. Grandma smiled.

You could hear Pudge Mullally squirming in the last pew as Moncrieff ascended to the pulpit. He took a moment to glare at Pudge, then clasped his palms over his chest and began softly:

"It is under a troubling sky, brothers and sisters, that we gather here today." There were murmurs of agreement. "The events of the past week have cast in question many of our lives' most precious activities." There were nods of approval, though not in our pew.

"Yet as so often, God has sent us a message within the message, a ship within the bottle bobbing on the waves." Grandma and Doc Crocker looked at each other.

"It behooves us to dwell on the deeper meaning of the notices received this week, to reflect on what is transitory and what is fundamental." Moncrieff shot a look around the hall.

"I have heard it said that for some of our friends and neighbors, the letters announcing the moving day have seemed a bolt from the blue." He paused and gripped the pulpit on either side, for emphasis. "Nothing could be further from the truth. Not only were these steps well known and advertised in advance by our elected leaders"—an unctuous bow to Lawyer Kincaid in the front row—"but at bottom, it matters not a pennywhistle where in God's village we make our abode—next to what tree, on what lane, in what hamlet." He stopped again, looked around, drew breath. The congregation seemed puzzled now.

———

"What does matter, what does matter a great deal, is that while we are residents of God's village we shall not give offense to him by willful acts contemptuous of his offices on earth." Moncrieff was in his element now: anger.

"The truly alarming announcement in the notices received this week had nothing to do with the happenstance of where, among all his creations, we shall each of us make our temporary home. No, it was the suggestion—the declaration—that *God's* homes on earth—his pews, his pulpits, his churches, *this building*—may be sold to the highest bidder, like slaves of old, thereafter to be treated as private property at the whim of the buyer at auction. *God's* offices are not private property, they are not to be treated as private property. The suggestion is nothing short of blasphemy, and it shall not stand!"

That Sunday was the last anyone worshiped in the Ripton church. Either Preacher Moncrieff got his wish or his enemies got their wish, because at four in the morning that Thursday, the town awoke to find the beautiful clapboard building entirely involved in flames. The volunteer fire department got their engine up the hill, but by that time the church was an inferno. There was nothing for it but to water down the surrounding area and the nearest buildings, to prevent the spread of the fire. This they succeeded in doing, as the massive structure was set well off from its neighbors. While the whole town looked on, the Ripton Congregational Church in the chill of a February daybreak burned to a fine ash. When we arrived, at around 7 A.M., there was a large and fascinated crowd, including both Hannah and Caleb. The only structure standing was the chimney of the parish house.

———

"I hope they got their things out of the basement," Hannah whispered to me.

"Who?"

"You know who."

"Oh, sure," I said.

Uncle Ed went up to Preacher Moncrieff and Clayton Hawley. "Have you seen the Mullally family here?" he asked.

"Not since Sunday," said Moncrieff.

"Were any of the men from Irishtown here on Sunday?"

"No, they have that dance hall in Greenwich."

Uncle Ed smiled at this. "What will you do now, Charles? Back to Worcester, or Boston?"

Moncrieff shook his head. "No, Worcester was filled when I left, and there's nothing in Boston. I will have to confer with the church authorities. There is no guarantee I shall stay in Massachusetts, though I must say I do have the feeling my work here is far from done."

Two weeks later, the Congregational Church announced the retirement of Reverend Cecil Wray, and assigned the parish at Enfield to Charles Moncrieff.

Spring

LIFE in the Valley slowed to a crawl in February. The cold had man and animal in its grip. I had not even the pleasure of a holiday, as Washington's birthday was not celebrated in our house. Grandma's family had not forgotten his assessment of Captain Shays in 1787.

The one time all year that the calendar made a difference to me was when March came in. No matter how cold it was, on March 1 we would set out to tap the maples. When we had a pint of syrup, we set it over the fire. As soon as it boiled we took it outside to pour on the snow. Since the snow was fresh, this produced a hiss, as the syrup congealed into maple "angels"—superior to any taffy or candy I ever bought in a store, then or since, even at the big emporiums in Worcester and Pittsfield.

Later in March Caleb and I went with Hammy to Rattlesnake Hill to catch the timber rattlers while they were still groggy from their hibernation. If you moved quickly and your nerve didn't fail you, they were easy to handle at that time of year. We would pin the snakes down with a forked stick and scrape them into a bag—oilskin, not burlap. Hammy directed us to an old man in Palmer who stuffed animals for a living. His premises reeked of formaldehyde. He paid us two dollars apiece for the live specimens. We did not untie the bags when we got to this store, because by then the critters inside had awakened and were in surly moods. The old man must have trusted us: he threw the sacks into a large icebox without even inspecting his merchandise. I mentioned this to Hammy, who chuckled and said that Caleb and I must have honest faces.

The end of March was the worst part of the year: mud season. You could travel only on horseback, at the side of the road and often enough a few yards into the woods. Any wagon or buckboard would be lost up to the top of its wheels in a matter of yards. The thawing created mud pits in the open fields, too, as dangerous as quicksand, accounting for the permanent disappearance of more than one favorite family pet. Even the venerated beagle belonging to the Bennett family lost his bearings and suffocated in this manner, partway between the Bennett farm and Ripton Centre. He must have dragged himself out before succumbing, as his muddy form was discovered on hard ground.

———

———

T H E district court of the commonwealth of Massachusetts sat at Orange, at the north end of the Valley, once a month from February to May. Other than that, the leadership in Boston had evidently concluded we had little need for intervention.

Grandma encouraged me and Hannah to jump on a Rabbit Railroad northbound, with or without fares, in order to attend the March sitting. "I don't remember ever learning anything in a courthouse," she said, "excepting that there are a lot of folks in a worse-off way than I am, and I was glad of it. Three times I've been on a jury, and twice I was a witness to goings-on about town and had to hang around the court for days on end, waiting to be called. I went home on every occasion and declared all courts to be a waste of time. It's as though they set out to punish everybody for coming near the court in the first place, by making the system as inefficient and unfair as they possibly can. And yet," she said, "every time, I believe I learned a lot that I didn't realize I was learning. You owe it to yourself to have seen it."

"It sounds like school. How will I recognize it when I see it?" I asked. Grandma waved away the question.

"The first time I was on a jury I was so het up and lathered that these two families had brought their dispute into public, I wanted to find against both of them. But eventually, after they make you sit through endless palaver, you realize there has to be an answer, and a court is as good a place as any to get it. They make it slow and tedious so folks will be numb and by the time anything is decided, they won't have the energy to kill each other, the way they would in a barroom."

I was not sure whether Grandma was serious about her theories on the judiciary, but it didn't matter. The important point to me and Hannah was the day out of school and the two train rides on a weekday.

Hannah insisted that we hop a train that got us to Orange around a quarter to nine in the morning, even though the bailiff would not bang his stick until ten.

"The best part is out in the street, before the proceedings begin," said Hannah. "You learn more then."

"How is that?"

"People let their guard down, so the falsity is more in the open."

I knew there was something wrong, or at least something special, as soon as the train slowed down for the stop at Orange station. There were three times as many people as I had ever seen on the platform. They weren't waiting for the train: they were milling about, bumping into one another. The ladies wore bustles. The men had homburgs and fedoras clamped on their heads. It was like a wedding or a funeral. Wagons choked the street and automobiles were parked all the way up to the courthouse.

The courtroom had railings of polished oak and benches of scrolled mahogany. The proceedings were incomprehensible and entertaining. Even when the clerk was droning on and on, there was usually somebody in the room who wanted him to get on to something else, and you could watch the color rise in that fellow's cheeks. Hannah and I made bets about how long it would be before the impatient one would make an outward sign such as tapping on the bench, or lose control altogether and give in to an outburst. Generally they didn't hold out as long as we had allowed them.

We had to stand at the back of the courtroom, as every seat on the benches was taken. The court officer asked me how old we were when we came in the room. I told him eighteen, which was not the case, but he moved on, as he apparently needed only an answer, not the truth. That was my first lesson in the law.

The front pews were occupied by anxious-looking folks dressed in their Sunday best, the back pews by regular court watchers and what I would describe as a barroom crowd, leering and elbowing one another in anticipation of the day's activities.

At ten o'clock, the preliminary agenda evidently exhausted, the clerk rose and boomed out, "Hear ye! Hear ye! All persons having anything to do before the honorable, the justices of the district court of the commonwealth, holden in and for the town of Orange, county of Franklin, draw near, give your attention, and you shall be heard." This struck me as strange because if one thing was clear, it was that nobody in that building had anything to do that day except to hang around and watch. In any event, these words signaled the approach of Judge Seabury, who seemed to take forever to ascend the staircase to his position.

Judge Seabury wore a black robe buttoned to his chin. Under the robe you could see he was bent over almost halfway, so his head preceded the rest of him by a couple of feet. He had a hunchback. There were creases of pain around his eyes from the moment he shuffled into court from behind a curtain until the moment he shuffled through the curtain behind his pulpit for frequent recesses.

Grandma had said that closer to the time of Captain Shays, in the eighteen hundreds, folks were so glad to be rid of the British and their powdered wigs that our judges didn't wear robes at all, just came out and sat in front of the litigants wearing a coat and necktie. No pulpit, either: those old judges would sit on a bench facing the other folks who had business before the court. I thought that sounded like a better system, but I was glad Judge Seabury had a gown so we wouldn't be exposed to the details of his locomotion.

"Commonwealth versus Tiverton, Houlihan, and Gilroy," the clerk intoned, and you could have heard a pin drop in the chamber. All eyes were on a woman and two men in the front pew.

"Well," said the judge at length, "what have we here, Mr. Fitzgibbons?"

Mr. Fitzgibbons was the district attorney for all of Franklin and Hampshire Counties, and well aware of that fact. He was a man the shape of an egg, no more than five feet tall and two hundred pounds if he was an ounce. He had a handsome smooth face with reddish brown hair cut close, a mustache, and a goatee that he kept waxed. His eyebrows arched up, his nose curved down, and his tiny mouth was a perfect rosebud circle. The goatee invited attention downward, to a belly straining the fabric of his vest even though the three bottom buttons were left unbuttoned. He carried a gold watch in a vest pocket, and a substantial gold fob (with which he played whenever addressing the court) at the end of the watch chain. He rose in a professional manner, without swagger, and addressed the court.

"A most regrettable circumstance, Your Honor. A disorderly house, uncovered by the unstinting efforts of Sergeants Beckett and Brannigan, working undercover, who penetrated the scheme. In the heart of Greenwich."

"Ouch!" said the judge. "Undercover, eh? What witnesses have you today beyond the detectives?"

"Just those, Your Honor. The case is to be bound over for the grand jury at next month's session."

At this point one of the lawyers for the defendants jumped to his feet.

"With all deference, Your Honor, whether the case is to be bound over for the grand jury is the question presented for Your Honor's consideration this morning, not a matter whose conclusion is to be assumed by the distinguished district attorney or anyone else."

"I understand that, I understand that," said Judge Seabury. "Why don't we hear from our two sergeants and you fellows can decide whether to expose these"—he now inspected the defendants, peering down over his spectacles—"objects of innocence to the vicissitudes of cross-examination."

"Very good, Your Honor," said the lawyer, and shot down into his place.

The district attorney made a speech, using the words "disorderly house," "lewd and lascivious," "affront to public decency," and even "crime against nature."

At the last phrase the judge interjected: "Technically?"

"Not technically, Your Honor, but in general," replied the district attorney.

"I see," said the judge, polishing his spectacles with a handkerchief.

The two sergeant detectives, sworn, recounted that they had entered the house of one Millie Tiverton and found six or seven ladies, elegantly costumed, fanning themselves in the living room, early on a Saturday evening.

"This is a crime?" asked Judge Seabury.

"Well, Your Honor, it was perfectly obvious what they were up to," testified Sergeant Beckett.

Hannah whispered, "I wonder if Ettie Clark was there. She's a friend of Millie." I pretended I had not heard.

"Go on," said the judge, waiting.

"We said we were there for business, but they would only offer us something to drink, and giggle. Then finally we said we were there for love, and they said they did not love us, but if we would stay downstairs, they would sell us a drink," said Sergeant Beckett.

"Fascinating. What then transpired?" asked the judge.

"We went upstairs, expecting the worst, and found room upon room containing beds," said the sergeant.

"Were you invited upstairs?"

"No sir, certainly not," said Beckett indignantly. At the government's counsel table, Fitzgibbons leaned over and said something to the other detective.

"I see," said the judge. "Did you have a warrant?"

The other detective stood. "No, but we were invited."

"You will have your opportunity, Sergeant Brannigan,"

———

said Seabury. "Well, I suppose it's not the first time a bed has made its way to a second story. One question for you, Mr. Beckett: may I infer that 'expecting the worst' means you had your weapons drawn?"

Beckett looked around at Brannigan, who looked at Fitzgibbons, who nodded. "Yes, of course, sir," said Beckett. He looked around again at the district attorney, who nodded slightly.

"And there were men and women running all about, out of the rooms and down the stairs, some with their suspenders undone or their nightshirts flapping, and you never saw such a scene!" he concluded. There was a roar from the back benches. In the third row a number of young men with pads and pencils were guffawing and taking notes as quickly as they could.

The judge arched his back and grimaced. He sat for half a minute while the tumult died down. Then he asked, "So, Mr. District Attorney, the charge is giggling, or unfastened suspenders, or loosed nightshirts, or some other charge?"

"Disorderly house, Your Honor," said Fitzgibbons, rising again with perfect punctilio and respect. "Chapter two seventy-two, section twenty-four."

"Recessed," said the judge, pounding with his gavel in the first display of force I had seen from him.

I had to go back to the farm at noon to help Francis Perrault with a load of lumber, so I left as soon as the recess was declared. I was envious of Hannah, who got to stay. I would have paid money to have heard from the lady with the high bonnet and the red cheeks, sitting in the front row, whom I took to be Millie Tiverton.

On the train ride back to Enfield I could think of only one thing, a matter that I had put out of my mind for months: my intimacy with Ettie Clark. Since that afternoon she had behaved with natural manners toward me, and I had had no desire to return to her room. The physical details of the encounter were blotted from my memory; I was merely aware that it had occurred, and thought of it as a shocking, isolated episode, as I would a death in the family.

Now, however, the leaves at the bottom of the lake had been stirred up. I had assumed that Ettie's experience with me must have been her first with a man. I saw this was ridiculous. She was a grown woman of twenty-four. More to the point, horridly to the point, she was a friend of Millie Tiverton, the now notorious Millie Tiverton! I pressed my eyes shut.

There I was in the dock. Judge Seabury and Sergeants Beckett and Brannigan were pointing at me. The bench was wobbling. There was a shriek. I shook my head and was awake on the train. Other passengers were near me. They might ask me questions. I closed my eyes again.

I saw Miss Ettie's auburn hair pulled back on her head, so her cheekbones were thrown out. She was at some work. I walked up behind her. She started like a doe.

Ettie and I were wandering along a dim hall in a castle. There were oil paintings on the walls, and torches in brackets. We were looking for something. There was a knocking from below. I dropped to my knees and searched for a trapdoor. It was not there. Beneath our feet, Hannah was skipping along a riverbed of dry stones. She was dressed in a dirndl, with puffy sleeves.

Phineas Neptune had to shake me awake. "Last stop, young man."

I was glad for the chance to help Francis with the lumber. I busied myself outdoors all afternoon, so as to avoid cross-examination by Grandma as to the day's activities.

Hannah returned at four-thirty. She said there had been no further testimony, only arguments between the judge and the lawyers that nobody could hear. Finally the clerk announced the case was put over until the next session. Millie and the two men left through a side door.

"The only people who were happy were the boys with the pads and pencils," Hannah said.

———

T H E next morning was dark. There had been a downpour. Hannah and I walked into the woods. Pools of rainwater mingled with the overflow eddies of Egypt Brook. The bark of trees was cold to the touch. There was some yellow from the willows and green buds on the thornbushes, but the predominant color was still black. Many trees and vines were split and bent over, as though a great upheaval had worked its way through the gully. That was the mark of ice storms months earlier. The slow-moving black water swept over smooth rocks topped with matted weed. On the bank, a few grasses were pushing through. A large dome of mud—surely the castle of some lucky creature—bore a snug roof of yellow moss. Last year's dead grasses had turned to straw, · their roots still holding to the ground.

I felt as though we were in the presence of some force.

———

"This is a civilization," I said. "That could be Mount Zion."

"It's been abandoned," said Hannah. "All the life and color got bled out of it. They'll be back, though."

"Let's come here with Potter Oakes and Will Grain on the fifteenth," I said.

"I thought you all went down School House Brook that day. Isn't that the opening of trout season?"

I felt myself redden. I picked up a long stick and poked in the mud with it. "We can do both," I said.

———

W H E N we returned to those woods a few weeks later with Will and Potter, we were unable to find the same spot. The stark landscape of mud and straw was gone, lime green grasses and ferns were up, and the swampy eddy had turned into a well-defined current, fringed by blue and yellow iris. A hummingbird's immobile blur seemed caught in the throat of a cardinal flower. He sped off sideways at our approach.

"Your miniature civilization is gone," said Hannah. "This is full-size now."

"Let's hope the fish are too," said Will Grain. This was our cue to pick up the pace toward School House Brook.

There was a lazy stream you had to cross to get to the School House. It made a big curve under a willow before falling down toward the mill house by a circuitous route. Hannah was first as we came up to the bend. A few yards from the water she doubled back, holding up ten fingers in front of her, then hooking her thumb back toward the stream.

"They're stacked up like cordwood," she whispered.

———

"Not in there," said Will Grain. "That water's six inches deep. A great blue would pick any trout out of there in minutes."

"I can see them."

"I'm not saying they aren't fish." To be on the safe side, Will and Potter pulled their flies off the cork and got the leader clear of the rod tip, then made false casts as they moved toward the stream a few inches at a time. If Hannah was right and there were trout there, they would see a Mickey Finn and a red-and-white bucktail before they saw Potter and Will.

"Suckers," said Will as they approached the spot where Hannah had turned. "There they go."

Hannah and I hurried up to take our own evidence. A few fish were still in fire-drill mode, racing around. Hannah grabbed my arm.

"Are they trout?"

"No, look at that, they've got their mouth on the bottom. That's how you can tell suckers. Those little ones over there, moving faster, are either dace or shiners, I can't tell from above."

Hannah turned to Potter and Will. "Some of those suckers were a foot long. Can you catch them?"

"They generally won't take a fly," said Potter.

"They never will take a fly," said Will. "All they eat is green scum."

"They're vegetarians?" said Hannah.

"Whatever," said Will, hooking his bucktail back into the cork and taking off for the brook at a trot. We fell in behind. In a few minutes I could hear the ripples where the brook first broke ground and began its pell-mell race to the mill pool.

For the first two hundred yards, School House Brook was too shallow to fish, so we picked our way downhill over rotting logs, leftover leaves, and light green moss. Will and Potter kicked at the skunk cabbage and knocked at jack-in-the-pulpits with their free hands, to see them spring back. Even they, however, took care to leave no impression on the forget-me-nots and tender masses of sweet william that lined our way.

Once I had to circle back for Hannah, who was conducting an inspection tour of bluets and lilies of the valley. "Come on!" said Will. "She's tying her shoelace," I said. When he turned to deal with the top of his fly rod, tangled in a pine branch, I picked a purple violet and pressed it into Hannah's hand.

"Thank you so much," she whispered. Her fist closed.

At the first considerable pool Will coaxed a nine-inch brook trout out from under a fallen birch. He struck its head on a rock. "Now back for your big brother," he said. Potter Oakes stood beside us, making no move toward the pool.

"Is that a small one?" Hannah whispered to me.

"You never throw back the first fish of the season, or even of the day. It's the worstest kind of luck."

"He did seem to be trying awfully hard to get away," said Hannah.

"Nuts!" said Will. His fly had snapped off midcast in a spruce, well over his head. He set his rod down at an angle on some berry bushes and trod around the tree, to judge the best branches for climbing. Extra bucktails were not a staple in Valley households.

Now Potter Oakes uncorked his small orange-and-yellow fly and made his way around the fast water at the top to the other side of the pool. "No barb, so I'll have to play 'em easy," he said. "Lost it on a rock in September."

He cast into the top of the pool, almost to the spot where Will Grain had been standing to reach the birch. Will by now was returning with his bucktail between his teeth.

"What are you doing there?" he said. "There's no water there."

"There's a falloff you can't see. There's no water right here, but if it swings down—"

Hannah screamed as the surface of the water gave way. Before there was any splash, I was conscious of a head, then a dorsal fin, then a surge of black water and a tail, straight out of water like a whale's. Potter's rod seemed on the point of snapping as the line danced toward the bottom of the pool. Potter hammered at the reel with the palm of his hand, to try to slow its revolutions. Below the fallen birch, halfway to the next pool, a golden arm plunged straight up out of the stream and slammed back again.

"There's another one!" Will shouted.

"That's him," said Potter, reeling in his slack line. "At least, that was him. I never had a chance, once he got under the birch."

"He's not for this tackle," I said. "He's for another day."

"I'd like to be here on that day," said Potter, examining the end of the line. The leader had snapped.

"So would I," said Hannah. "That was beautiful, Potter." Potter managed a smile. "At least it wasn't the barb," he said.

"I've got two Mickey Finns and a gray ghost at the farm," I

said, "stuck in a beam in the attic. Let's make sure we're equipped for tomorrow, anyway." No one raised any objection, and we trudged off. I couldn't get the golden arm out of my mind. It had to be a brook trout, a native, probably four pounds. I felt that I had been part of something important.

———

Doc Crocker and Preacher Moncrieff were sitting in the front room when we came in and made for the stairs.

"Jamieson Kooby! Come in and say hello to your elders and your betters. And introduce your friends."

"Yes, Grandma." I turned to lead the party in, and saw Will Grain's heels already at the top of the stairs, making not a sound. So one had escaped.

"Doc, how are you? Preacher. This is Hannah. And Potter." Doc Crocker was smoking a cigarette and drinking from a dark green glass, Moncrieff smoking a cigar, which he now removed.

"You're Throop Oakes's boy, aren't you?" said Moncrieff.

"Yes sir. Well, people call him Trembly."

"Why is that?"

"It's just a nickname," said Doc Crocker, pouring himself another drink from an unmarked brown bottle. "He's had it since he was a boy."

"Yes, he's always had it," said Grandma.

"We'll have to get you an index of some sort, to help you sort out your flock," Doc Crocker said, then collapsed in a coughing fit.

Preacher Moncrieff looked at Doc Crocker without saying

———

anything. I thought his jaw hardened a little. Then he spoke up but did not raise his voice.

"I'm well aware I'm new to the Valley. That's the nature of my work. I answer to others. You, sir, if I may"—he extended his right arm and pointed his finger at Doc Crocker, almost close enough to tap him on the chest—"where I am a man of the cloth, you are supposed to be a man of health. Yet you drink spirits and smoke those cigarettes all day. You went to medical training for five years, even if it was in New Orleans. You must have had willpower and discipline then. Why don't we see them now?"

Doc Crocker set his glass down. "I've got discipline, and willpower if I want it. There's certain places I don't care to go, is the only thing."

"He came back," said Grandma to Preacher Moncrieff. "We're grateful he came back."

"I'll grant you that," said Moncrieff, surveying and tapping the ash of his cigar. He looked back at Doc Crocker.

"Why do you drink?" he said.

"It keeps me hopeful."

"What does that mean?"

"It makes me forget the savagery which lurks beneath the surface of many organized activities."

"Such as what?"

Doc Crocker stared at Moncrieff for a moment. "Such as civilization," he said. Moncrieff nodded, but you could still see his jawline.

"I can think of others," said Grandma.

Doc Crocker took another swig from his glass, choked on it, and fell to coughing again.

———

"Look at you, you're half dead," said Moncrieff.

"At least I'm half alive," said Doc Crocker. Grandma and the preacher laughed at this.

"Everything in moderation, especially moderation," said Grandma. We slipped out and stole up to the attic. I don't think they noticed us, as they had quite a full plate by that point.

―――――

CALEB Durand shared my obsession to possess in hand the specimens of nature, animate as well as inert. This usually required a preliminary exercise, that is, killing the bird or fish or animal in question. I left my air rifle at home when I went out with Caleb, since he did not have one, but we made out fine with our slingshots.

On a chilly April morning we came upon three robins in a field, each of whom was tugging up inches of fat, resistant earthworm. As I was admiring the spectacle I became aware that Caleb was aiming his sling at the birds.

"Don't!" I shouted.

"Why not? Since when did you ever not want to kill a bird?"

This was a fair question, and I was momentarily befuddled. But a glance at the busy and oblivious robins inspired me: "It's more important that the night crawlers die. They're halfway through it anyway."

Caleb was persuaded by this, and the robins were spared.

The one bird we could never seem to reduce to our possession was the crow. If we didn't have our slingshots they

―――――

would ignore us, even if we made gestures as though to strangle them. But if we were armed, their sentinels would spot us half a mile away and raise an alarm that echoed from Mount Lizzie to Mount L.

Caleb's family maintained a front room whose shelves boasted stuffed specimens of many species, feathered and furred. The crown jewel of the collection, at the center of the highest shelf, was a great horned owl. Its shoulders had been pierced and fitted with two ten-foot lengths of household cord, so that by pulling the cord from below you could make the owl's wings flap.

The only time we ever succeeded in doing damage to the crow population of our county was when we borrowed this magnificent creature and wedged its base in the crook of an oak tree, six feet above the ground. We had spent the better part of two mornings creating a blind of sharpened ash and basswood branches at the bottom of the oak. Here we secreted ourselves from one until four in the afternoon, making neither a motion nor a sound. Not a crow in sight. No cawing in the distance, either. The entire crow population of Franklin and Hampshire Counties evidently had decamped to pursue other opportunities.

Caleb looked at me pleadingly. Almost without moving his lips he mouthed the word "Now?" I nodded. Each of us, moving a thumb and forefinger just a few inches, grasped the end of a length of household cord and drew it down. The great horned owl flapped its wings once, twice.

The hills around us were instantly alive with shrieks of outrage, the air thick with black suicide dive-bombers. Crows were in our faces, crows were in the branches above us,

crows plunged straight into our palisade of ash and basswood, prying its members apart. There must have been four
hundred crows watching that owl for hours, invisibly, silent-
ly, waiting for a sign as to whether it was the hated genuine
article. Beyond human patience, beyond human discipline.

Caleb and I jumped to our feet.

"Get them or they'll kill us!" he shouted. I fumbled with
my ammunition. As I bent to retrieve the stone I saw Caleb
let fly and strike one of the smaller crows in the breast at
point-blank range. She collapsed onto the ground on her back
but quickly righted herself and began hopping away from us,
on one foot.

"Shoot!" said Caleb. "Shoot for God's sake!"

I shot hurriedly. My heart lifted as I saw I had missed the
miserable bird.

Caleb's second shot kicked up the dust under the crow's
carriage, which induced her to spring awkwardly into the air
and flap a bit. She looked as though she could no more make
a sustained go of it than our mummified great horned owl.
Then an amazing thing happened.

Four larger crows swooped down in unison and scooped
the wounded bird onto their mass. As she continued to flap
feebly, they soared off together in such close formation that it
appeared the wounded crow was being borne on the backs of
the others. They disappeared into the foliage at the top of a
huge beech, out of slingshot range from any vantage point.
Then the silence descended again and not a crow was to be
seen. It was as though a maestro had waved a wand.

That was the last time I shot at a crow. Or wanted to shoot
a crow. I kept this from Caleb, as I knew there was no

prospect of persuading him and was not even sure what had induced my own change in attitude.

———

T H E flooding of the Valley still seemed unreal and remote, but nature gave us an appetizer in late spring, when the wide beaver dam at the outlet of Darey Pond gave way after heavy rains. It was as though you had roused a sleeping tiger and opened the door to its cage: the dammed lake sprang down the course of Beaver Brook, sweeping trees and houses carelessly before it. A waterborne 1932 Dodge DeSoto hit the granite at the lower end of Great Falls at forty miles an hour and exploded into unrecognizable shrapnel. For two months after the flood, the fields on either side of Beaver Brook were treasure troves for the boys of Ripton and Enfield. Eventually we picked them clean. Caleb and I made red-and-green sculptures out of bits of farm machinery. I kept mine in the attic. Caleb installed his right outside the front door of their house. "It's the first thing we're going to move," he said.

"Move where?"

"We don't know yet, but you know, when we have to move. In the fall."

"Oh. Sure." In fact I had not thought of the impending change since the week the Ripton church burned down.

At dinner that evening I asked Grandma where we were going to move. This produced a lengthy silence, which was unlike her. At first I thought her mouth was full. When I saw she was not chewing, I laid down my knife and fork and waited.

"I prefer to think of the question as whether we are going

———

to move, not where we are going to move," she said. "The jury is still out on a few issues."

"Sounds good to me," I said.

But as Grandma and I whistled past the graveyard, events were rolling on without us.

———

In order to clear the Valley in preparation for the flooding, Governor James Michael Curley sent out hundreds of unskilled men from Boston. They did not know one end of a saw or hoe from another and were as like to cut their foot or toes off as to cut a tree. Grandma said Curley needed them to be paid, that they were the men who had twice elected him mayor of Boston and then governor of the commonwealth. The Woodpeckers, as they were called in the Valley, caused a hardening of anti-Irish sentiment. Virtually every one of them spoke with a brogue, and if you could understand them, they made little sense, most of them. You still hear people say today that we have curbstones in western Massachusetts hill towns that Curley's Woodpeckers laid out in fields where there were no roads.

Caleb and I took Pudge Mullally on weekends to observe the Woodpecker crews at their work. It was entertaining, at least while they were getting the hang of the equipment. When they were trying to clear a field in Ripton Flats, one gigantic man without a shirt struggled for the better part of an hour to get a scythe working for him. He was sweating furiously, but at least he seemed more angry at himself than at the tool. Caleb and I approached him.

———

"Let me try to give that a swing," said Caleb. He showed the proper form and soon had made a substantial dent in the standing grain. The giant was openmouthed.

"There's no magic," said Caleb. "You either know it or you don't. Here." He put the scythe in the man's hands and guided him through a few strokes.

"I'm much obliged," said the man, putting out his hand. "My name is Eustace Weller." We introduced ourselves.

"And who are you?" he said to Pudge, leaning over and extending a massive arm. "My name's Eustace."

Pudge opened up. "Pudge. Pudge Mullally."

"Mullally? Well, if that isn't a fine broth of a name! You could be one of mine," he said, mussing Pudge's hair with a paw. "I've got one like you at home. In fact I've got seven like you at home."

The early weeks of clearing saw the three of us, and particularly Pudge, hanging around the work crews a good deal. When Eustace had a break, Pudge traipsed behind him as he went to see how the men in his crew had been getting along. After a while Pudge developed, on a tiny scale, the same lope as Eustace. It was enough to make you smile. "Think he would do that at home?" said Caleb. Caleb had a way of coming straight to the point.

Eustace told us quite a bit about James Michael Curley, the mayor and governor. It was a different picture from Grandma's.

"He's the least selfish man I've ever met, the truest friend of the poor, and he has half the state set against him," said Eustace. "People are scared of the poor, they hate the poor, and so they fear and hate the greatest man in Massachusetts."

"The people in the west don't think we need the people

from the east to come out and put our towns underwater," said Caleb.

"Curley's enemies always seek to divide his friends and natural allies," said Eustace, sitting down on a log to put his face closer to ours. He put his arm around Pudge, who was at rapt attention. "It's not east versus west you should be thinking, it's rich versus poor. If it weren't for Curley, there would be no hospital for the poor in Boston. There would be no food on the table, and no end of disease, in the tenements of the North End."

"It's rich versus poor," said Pudge.

"What about our farms?" said Caleb.

Eustace put up his palms. "There will be other farms," he said. "If we can elect Curley governor once again, there will be farms for everyone." He patted Pudge on the back.

"That's right," said Pudge.

———

E U S T A C E Weller was promoted to be in charge of all the demolition work when his supervisor, Michael O'Hara, returned to Boston. O'Hara had been billeted on the third floor of a boardinghouse in Prescott, near the poor farm. He acted crotchety and looked haggard the first two days on the job, as though he hadn't had much sleep, and the third morning ran from the house. He caught the 8:17 A.M. from Orange to Boston and never came back. Eustace said he was surprised, O'Hara had always been a proud man and a good worker. Hannah said she was not at all surprised, and told me the history of the place.

———

A young man named MacGregor, from Utica, New York, had stayed in that room on the third floor for a month in the 1880s, while paying court to Pamela Renwick of Prescott. They were devoted to each other. She was the daughter of a well-to-do family. One day MacGregor disappeared. For reasons known best to herself, Miss Renwick promptly committed suicide by cutting off her right hand on the motorized saw in her father's mill during the men's luncheon shift. She carried the hand to the back room, dropped it out the window into the flume below, and remained there noiselessly when the men returned from lunch, till fainting and then expiring from loss of blood. It cost the foreman his job. It was Friday and the men had enjoyed a few grogs, so no one noticed the blood on the saw or thought to investigate, and the lovesick girl got her way.

The suite on the third floor was shuttered for a year, but after Mr. Renwick sold his mill and moved away from the Valley and its unhappy memories, the room was reopened to the traveling public. It was used principally for travelers from afar.

The first overnight visitor, a plump tobacco factor from Manchester, England, who was conducting an inspection tour, complained of difficulty breathing in his sleep. No one said a word to him except by way of commiseration.

Jebediah Speed of Charleston, South Carolina, was the first visitor to report that something had brushed across his face while he was sleeping. He judged it had been the silk coverlet, stirred by the wind, and did not make much of it.

Later tenants of the third floor were more precise. They swore they had been awakened by the touch of a human hand running across their face, though no one ever found another soul in the room on lighting the candle or, later, the electric light.

To Hannah it was simple. Pamela Renwick, acting through the only instrumentality she retained above ground, wished to determine whether her lover might have returned.

I wasn't sure about that, but I do know this: when Curley's Woodpeckers tried to demolish that boardinghouse in Prescott, they found they could not rip it down with all the adzes and sledgehammers and crowbars in Massachusetts. Eustace Weller said it was because chestnut wood will hold a nail extra well. They wound up burning the place to the ground. The wood timbers shrieked the way a pine log with water in it will do in a fire. Even though, as I pointed out to Eustace, there wasn't one loose knot or crevice in all those chestnut timbers.

———

THE daily presence of the Woodpeckers in the Valley made it far more difficult to wish away what was going to happen to us. You could see the strain beginning to settle in on people, particularly when they were together in groups so they couldn't take refuge in their own wishful thoughts.

At the Sunday services in Enfield, Preacher Moncrieff thundered from the pulpit that it was the duty of the Valley residents to submit to the flooding plan as God's will. A number of the congregants did not take kindly to this.

"I'll tell you what's God's will," said Henry Houlihan, a fervent Irishman who had come to public attention as a result

———

of his visit to Millie Tiverton's. "The turn of the seasons is God's will. The leaves of a lettuce are God's will. A fox's burrow is God's will." People near him murmured concurrence.

Preacher Moncrieff gave no sign from the pulpit that he had heard a word of this, but a few minutes later he pinned Houlihan to his seat with a reminder of his courtroom notoriety.

"'There are many mansions in my Father's house,'" he quoted, then added, "but my Father would not keep a disorderly house."

After the service, Houlihan and his fellow defendant Gene Gilroy had words with Moncrieff in the back of the church. I slumped down in my pew so as not to be seen and dismissed.

"Those charges have all been put over by Judge Seabury, Preacher, and you know it!" said Houlihan.

"I see. Were they put over because they were untrue, or upon some procedural ground?"

Gilroy stepped between them. "Why don't you tell us what's really on your mind, sir, if something is bothering you."

"Nothing is bothering me. I have a responsibility toward my flock, to see they are not led into error."

Houlihan extended an arm behind him. "These are men and women, Father, not sheep."

Moncrieff smiled. "Evidently that seems to be at the root of the difficulty." Houlihan and Gilroy pushed past him into the sunlight.

I followed them out the double doors. A pale green luna moth moved uncertainly across the white clapboard and attached itself to the door latch. Pudge Mullally's eyes were on stalks. He pointed out the moth to Preacher Moncrieff, the last to emerge. Moncrieff said, "Oh. I see. It is a large one. But we've got to get on with it." He seized the latch with his thumb and forefinger, crushing the moth's wing. The moth fell to the ground as Moncrieff pushed the doors shut. "There," he said, rubbing the green dust off his hands. "Now, on to the next thing." He strode off.

Pudge went over to the moth, which was flopping on the ground. He picked it up gently and threw it hopefully into the air, but it never managed a full wing beat and fell to earth, landing on its back. It fluttered feebly but could not right itself. Pudge's mouth was working.

Caleb walked over and nudged the moth with the point of his shoe.

"He's not going anywhere, Pudge. Do you want me to step on him, so he won't suffer?"

Pudge turned away. "Yes," he said, and kept walking.

———

APRIL 27, 1938, was the date long since chosen for the town of Enfield's Celebration Ball, and all in town were determined to see it through. What we were celebrating that year was none too clear to me, but I judged it not my place to challenge the settled decisions of my elders: perhaps the ball would mark the beginning of a counteroffensive against the land takings.

Caleb and I, wearing our best trousers and long-sleeved shirts, and Hannah, in a frock borrowed from Annie Richards, lounged against the railing of the stairs to the front door of the

———

Town Hall. We were eager for the evening. Lawyer Kincaid and Preacher Moncrieff were standing just inside the door. Who should be the first family to arrive but the Hulces.

Annie Hulce, the daughter, was scared of her shadow. At twelve she was the tallest girl in the Enfield school, towering over boys two years her senior. She had curly blond hair, hazel eyes, and a certain athletic grace, despite having grown well beyond her social competence. She moved her shoulders from side to side as she walked, so as not to progress in a straightforward manner.

Annie's stepmother insisted on Annie wearing her white leather pump shoes, with straps, at the least provocation or pretext. On such occasions Annie would arrive purple with shame and rage. Generally she would make a show of gazing at the ceiling or the stars, hoping to draw the eyes of others upward. Tonight was no exception. We children, we cruel children, understood her discomfort.

"Annie! Nice shoes!" said Caleb as her foot probed the first step. She withdrew it and hurried off a few paces to gather herself. My stomach turned over.

"Give it a rest, Caleb," I said, poking him in the ribs with my elbow.

"You all are welcome to go in," I said to Annie and her father and stepmother. They did so.

"She's only twelve," I said when she was safely inside.

"She's as gawky as she can be," said Caleb.

"She's only twelve."

"Suit yourself, Romeo."

"Don't be ridiculous."

After an hour of superior loitering, we joined the party.

Inside the hall, black and white crepe was hung round the walls, and streamers taped to the ceiling. A man I didn't know was playing "Turkey in the Straw" on a fiddle, and a number of young swells and their girls were stomping their feet and clapping in time with the music. The older folks were sitting against the walls on folding wooden chairs. They mostly didn't have drinks in their hands, or much expression on their faces.

After a while the fellow with the fiddle gave it up and went over to Wilbur Hodge, who was tending bar, to try to cadge a drink. This created an unwelcome lull; the young people moved in a pack around the hall, seeking diversion. Uncle Ed Hardiman had been sitting on a piano stool, his back to a honky-tonk piano, watching the fiddler. He was wearing a boater, a striped shirt, and sleeve garters. No mourner he. All that was missing was the cane. No one had asked him to play until now, but the crowd was suddenly insistent. Youth must be served.

"Oh all right," he sighed, and wheeled his stool around. I judged he had been planning on this. He opened his mouth wide and popped his eyes as he accompanied himself:

De Camptown ladies sing dis song, doo-dah, doo-dah!
De Camptown racetrack five miles long, oh doo-dah day!
Gwine to run all night,
Gwine to run all day!
I'll bet my money on de bobtail nag,
Somebody bet on de bay.

This song roused even some of the spectators to tap their feet and stand. Carl Kincaid came over to clap Uncle Ed on the back and shake his hand after the last chorus, as though it was amazing anyone could play the piano. He turned to face the line of people against the wall.

"Ain't he something?" he said. His hand was still on Uncle Ed's shoulder, denoting possession.

———

Over the course of the evening, Lawyer Kincaid must have shaken the hand of every adult in the hall three times.

"What's he doing?" I asked Grandma as we were observing this ritual from across the ballroom floor.

"He's dancing his way back to the legislature, Jamieson. This is a kind of dance called campaigning."

"You don't mean people will vote for him just because he shakes their hand?"

Grandma shook her head and smiled. "Of course they will," she said. "Look at him and those old ladies."

Kincaid had his arm around the waist of a frail woman and a hand on the shoulder of her companion. "Now, girls," he said, "I won't hear of any more fussing. This is all for the best; we should all think of it as an opportunity, and be grateful for it."

"But where will I find a farm or a house like Hubert's?" asked the frail woman.

"It will all be for the best, Liza. I promise you. We shall see to that in the legislature."

"Well, I don't know," said her companion, "but I'm glad we've got you there in a position to help."

Lawyer Kincaid hooked his thumbs behind his suspenders. "That I am," he said, smiling. I noticed gold fillings

———

in his back teeth, top and bottom. No one else in town had gold fillings.

———

As the last months of our life in the Valley slipped by, the natural order began to go topsy-turvy. I should have known then that there would be no reprieve.

The ground just around our farmhouse was not planted. Grandma said it was a throwback to the Southern origins of the Hardiman family, where people would leave a bare stretch around the home so snakes couldn't creep up without being seen.

When we got a couple of hot days in April, all the bare ground began to crack and blister, even the part with some crabgrass. Hannah and I took note, and conducted an inspection tour.

"This is the beginning of the end of the world," said Hannah. "It's not hot enough to make the ground break. There's some other force in here."

"You've been listening too hard to Preacher Moncrieff," I said. "You think these little holes are sent from above? More likely some new kind of ant or something."

"Biggest ant I'd have ever seen," said Hannah. She took a stick and flicked it through a crabgrass patch. "What are these?" she said.

Two miniature skeletons like crayfish, except longer and narrower, lay nose to nose on the ground. They had the thorax of a grasshopper but more thickly plated, and under-appendages of some sort, like a centipede.

———

"Dinosaurs!" said Hannah.

I became aware of a droning sound and looked up quickly for hornets or yellow jackets, already calculating the shortest distance to the pond. Caleb and I had had seven hornet stings between us the previous summer, after approaching too close to a burning nest—how had it possibly caught fire? We had escaped only by swimming underwater in Goose Pond for lengthy stretches over an hour-long period.

The air was thick with creatures, not hornets or yellow jackets, closer to dragonflies. They seemed the clumsiest advance sentinels in history, many flying into tree trunks or branches and falling dead to the ground. We ran for the house.

"The end is near," said Grandma. "This is the scourge foretold of old. What have you two been up to?"

"Tell, Grandma."

"Those are seventeen-year locusts, Jamieson. Invasion from below, every seventeen years to the minute, then eggs back underground. They live only a day up top, molt those beautiful exoskeletons you saw. I wish I had a barrel."

Hannah and I looked at each other. "We have stuff at the poor farm we can use," she said. "In the shed." She sped off.

Hannah returned with four cans of paint from the farm: red, silver, green, and gold. We collected seven hundred of the cicada carcasses over the next three days, dipped every one into paint on a pin, and put a mixed hundred into each of seven mason jars after the paint dried. We cut holes in the tops of the jars, just as we did for live bats, because you don't want new paint to be enclosed in the summer, even if it has dried. The jars would have exploded.

———

The locusts were gone in a week. I was thankful they left their skeletons behind. Grandma teased Preacher Moncrieff about it after church. "How could the plague of the locusts have been so bad? This is no worse than the chickens coming home to roost," she said. Moncrieff said they were a different kind; the ones in the Bible were worse.

Grandma was not satisfied with this. "Were the wild animals in the Bible worse too?" she asked.

"Well, perhaps wilder," said Preacher Moncrieff. "It was an earlier time, a sinful and dangerous time."

"It certainly was dangerous," said Grandma. "They killed that poor servant who buried the seven talents of silver for safekeeping."

"They had to do that," said Moncrieff. Grandma was opening her mouth for another volley when I surprised myself by dragging her off. I was thinking of lunch.

I still have my jar of locusts. I keep it on my dresser, next to a photograph of a dead man standing against a tree, and a photograph of Hannah that I have.

———

M ANY of my possessions have become lovely with age, but the jar of locusts I thought beautiful from the beginning. It has glass and color, contours and contents, stillness and motion, a frenzy of activity captured and frozen.

The first time I set it down in my room, Hannah was standing with me.

"Those are your curled-up lives," I said. "You're nothing but a vessel."

———

"I used to have real experiences. It's only here with you that I'm nothing, I'm a glass of water. But you should talk, you with your curled-up life in this fertile valley."

I laughed. "Why are you called Hannah?" I said. I expected an answer, and got one.

"I was Hannah North. I was hanged as a witch at the Salem trials in sixteen ninety-two."

"Best not tell Preacher Moncrieff. He doesn't favor witches. Believes they confuse our notions of the living and the dead."

"Preacher Moncrieff has no further idea about the dead than he does about the living, which is no idea at all. The only thing I've ever heard him get right is 'On that day the dead shall be raised.' But he doesn't know what day it's going to be."

"When you hear the voices of people in the past, are you in a waking state? Can you pinch yourself and still hear them?"

"Of course you can still hear them. Pinching doesn't do anything. If you're looking out a window on a sunny day and you close your eyes, can't you still see the slats of wood?"

"Yes, but in a negative. They're white and the sky is black."

"Well, then." She went out of the room and left me thinking.

———

Four days after the Enfield ball, another civic event was upon our family. Every year on the first of May, Old Glory stayed folded in the garden shed, and hundreds of green and yellow streamers were wound round the brass ball at the top of the flagpole, hanging limp to the ground with plenty to spare. At the appointed signal from Grandma, all the children of the surrounding villages would dash in to take up a streamer and race around in circles to create the Maypole. Some ran clockwise and some counterclockwise; there was quite an art to making sure your streamer did not get fouled with a rival strand before wrapping all the way around the pole. The trick, in my experience, was to get as far away from the pole as possible, holding your line as high as possible, and then work in toward the pole.

On this occasion Hannah and I stood near Grandma and Doc Crocker and the preacher to observe. Without anyone telling me, I knew that I was now a graduate of the May Day exercises, not a participant. I invited Hannah to join in, but she declared she preferred to watch.

At noon precisely, Grandma rang the bell on the old locust tree. The children raced across the lawn, the younger ones so eager they used their arms as propellers. The threads were taken up, producing much screaming and confusion as the contestants ran smack into one another, which was the design of those in charge. Doc Crocker picked his way through the orbiting planets to help one of the littlest girls retrieve the end of her garland, which had fallen and been pulled away from her. She was trying not to cry. He got there just in time.

"Watch," said Hannah.

"I am," I said.

I heard the pipes before I saw the men. They must have run straight from the woods on the far side of the Maypole. There were three of them, dancing and cavorting around the outer edge of the children, barefoot and bare chested and painted green from waist to face. They wore close-fitting green caps—ladies' bathing caps, I supposed—and were covered with vines and leaves. They were certainly not skilled musicians, but their short pipes—one held to the front, two to the side—provided at least the rhythm, if not a melody, for their dance. The children stood stock-still as the three completed their circumference of the pole and sprinted back whence they had come. All cheered, and no one thought to follow them: the scene had been completed and was past.

I should say almost all cheered. As I sauntered over to Grandma to share my observations, Preacher Moncrieff was squatting down to pick up a lit cigar that had fallen out of his mouth. His neck was more purple than usual.

"Lose something, Preacher?" asked Hannah from behind me. Moncrieff looked up with a grunt, and there was I in the line of fire. I stepped to the side but his eye followed me. Placing a hand on his knee, he finally righted himself and puffed with a lover's intensity, seeking to resuscitate his cigar. No good, it had gone out. He shook it furiously, but there was no spark. I am afraid that the contrast between this enormous, worried man and his tiny inert cigar was almost too much for me. I was having difficulty composing my features when Moncrieff looked at me again.

"Yes, I've lost something. I've lost the opportunity to enjoy an innocent children's game without seeing it desecrated by sacrilege."

"Sacrifice?" said Hannah, having again maneuvered behind me.

"Sacrilege. That was a pagan dance, no mistaking it. All that was missing was the goats' feet, and those three would have been satyrs."

"Weren't they just boys enjoying themselves?" asked Grandma. "I thought they were quite good, quite athletic, even if they couldn't play a note."

"When you get to the point of formal celebration, Mrs. Hardiman, you must be careful of how things appear. It is not always wise to indulge one's appetite for pleasure or for self-expression. That may seem fine for oneself, but there are others to consider. There is the good of the whole."

"Is it the green paint that hurts the good of the whole, or the dancing?" These were impudent words, out of my mouth before I knew I was speaking. Moncrieff stared at me for a moment.

"It is the suggestion, Jamieson, that there are forces to be appealed to other than the Lord God Almighty. Any fool can worship a tree or a false icon. If people are encouraged to think such foolery can satisfy their spiritual needs, that is very much destructive to the good of the whole."

"Yes, I see, sir," I said. I was feeling guilty about having been too smart-alecky.

"The whole church," Hannah whispered in my ear.

———

On the last Sunday in May most of the folks left in the five towns gathered by the gun on Ripton Green to celebrate

———

Decoration Day. This had always seemed to me a pretty good show all around; the howitzer with its vast protective plate reminded me of an armored dinosaur, and had been the stuff of many an afternoon's fancy. Also, you never saw so many American flags.

Until this year I had not been quite clear on the concept. The emphasis for me had always fallen on decoration, rather than on death. True it was that the graveyard made a pretty sight, with rows of flags snapping to attention in the breeze. One of the town's leading citizens always made a patriotic speech to considerable cheering. I had always drunk in the spectacle and never listened to a word.

In 1938, Uncle Ed was the speaker. I made the mistake of listening. We were here to honor those who had sacrificed much. They had left their families and given all they had in order to protect our homes. They made the ultimate sacrifice so that we might live the lives we cherish so well, in these five towns, in our homes.

Now I looked and saw the gravestones, not the flags. Most of the stones had mildew and were worn; they were not cared for currently. The rows of flags, all alike and all planted with the same hand that morning to assure a line of military precision, seemed a candying over of the sacrifices buried four and six feet deep. The Enfield ball had celebrated the impending death of our towns. This ceremony celebrated the past death of its leading citizens.

The martial spirit rose in me. I quite forgot my stegosaurus and triceratops. I leaned over to whisper into Grandma's bonnet, "Who's sacrificing now?"

"Why, Jamieson Kooby, that's the first time you've ever bowed your head to speak to me. I declare you're a man." She beheld me with delight. I hesitated, forgetting my question.

"The answer, son, is that we are sacrificing, but the difference is that it's not our idea, and it's not saving our homes, because *they* are the sacrifice. The only thing that's the same is our own government is making us do it."

Pudge tugged at Grandma's sleeve, and she in turn bent down.

"Why do they have the party when the heroes are all dead?" he asked in an unsure voice.

"To remember the heroes."

"Like Captain Shays, Grandma?"

"Like Captain Shays."

———

NOT everyone, of course, was a leading citizen like Uncle Ed. Pudge Mullally's father, for example, was one of the lost souls of the Valley. Nobody much knew what he did for a living. But Caleb and I found out.

Off to the east of the quarry in Greenwich was a small mud pond, not good for catching much beyond minnows. It was a year-round pond, spring fed, but you couldn't see where the water let out unless you knew where to look. If you weren't scared of snapping turtles and spent time in the pond, you knew that the densest blueberry patches began halfway down the overhanging bank, invisible from above to man and bird alike, and that the easiest way to pick them was by treading

———

water, unless you could sneak an inner tube from a neighbor's barn.

The area was overgrown with brush and hawthorn. Caleb and I had cut a tunnel through the briers for fifty feet to permit access to the pond. We took care to cover up the tunnel mouth whenever we left. So far as we knew, it was never discovered. We were the only proprietors of the place, ever.

The outlet stream ran under rocks for twenty feet or so, then came up behind some bushes and made its way for half a mile down to an eddy of the Swift. The stream was shallow and clear, pebble bottom, and lined with watercress much of the way. It was icy cold almost all the year. Both banks were packed with huckleberry, dogberry, ground juniper, and alders, with plenty of brambles behind them.

On the morning after Decoration Day, I went to the cow pen behind the barn and scraped a number of cow pies off to a corner with my shovel. The earth here was as black and as soft as it could be, so even in bare feet I had no difficulty driving the blade of the shovel well in, or in turning it up. Two shovelfuls produced a dozen fine earthworms, not counting those who had been decapitated. I put these in a tin can, along with a generous supply of loam, and ran past the horse field before anyone could intercept me.

A mile and a half down the Palmer Road I encountered Caleb, sitting on a log and chewing a variety of grasses, like me wearing only a bathing suit.

We fell in together without a word and continued along the road toward the mud pond. What a pleasure there is in omitting any greeting!

―――

After a while we clambered up the bank on the left side of the road and across a field of fourth-growth timber to the tangle of brambles. At the end of our tunnel we lifted a thatch of matted grass and removed from their hiding place two rubber tubes from automobile tires and two long hand lines, each with a swivel, a single gold spinner, and a small treble gang hook.

From an old log we pried off flat pieces of wood, not yet too rotten, which would carry our cargo deep into enemy territory. We rolled the tubes from the lip of the pond across the slate outcropping to the spot where the stream rose to the surface. Here we fixed earthworms onto our treble hooks, taking care to drive one of the hooks cleanly through the reinforced ring. This would prevent a fish from tearing the worm free at the first nibble. We laid the hooks on two strips of bark, then unwound the entire length of the hand line from its frame, as you do not have time to do this once the wood starts floating downstream. The worm would be pulled off the wood prematurely, and you would have to start over. Needless to say the arrangement of the hand line in a coil that will pay out smoothly without snarling is a part of the high art of float fishing.

When all was in readiness, we placed our freighted craft in the first black water of the stream. Caleb's took off downstream smartly, but mine hit a stick and capsized almost immediately. This was vexing, since even though my second launch was successful, I knew that Caleb's earthworm would be twenty feet ahead of mine down the length of the stream. Twenty feet closer to the lair of the huge wild trout or bass. I was thinking of him. Was he thinking of me?

When Caleb's line had paid out he gave a tug to drop his

———

bait into the water. He had not hauled in three arm's lengths of line when he let out a yell. I reflexively tugged on my line, which cost me an extra fifteen or twenty feet of drifting. If you are concentrating on fishing or hunting, and someone says "Strike!" or "Shoot!" your reflexes take over. That is as it should be, because nine times out of ten, to hesitate is to lose the game. This was not one of those times. I cursed my earthworm.

Caleb pulled his fish in without finesse. With a hand line, as opposed to a pole, there is no opportunity to play the fish. A fishing pole prevents the fish from getting a direct pull at the reel. With a hand line, the force of the fight is not spread out over the length of a pole; it is direct. So you have to get the fish in fast, before he shakes his head so much that the hook tears out.

The fish was coming in easily, but you never know: it could be a big one swimming upstream. Thirty feet out it seemed to give up the fight and rose to the surface. A perfect circle broke water like a periscope.

"Largemouth," said Caleb disgustedly. He had been hoping for a trout. "Not that large either," he added.

A fillet of largemouth bass is a fine dish, particularly with a little lemon on it, but as we were not heading directly home, we released the bass to the stream. I held his gills open and ran him up and down the current a few times to get things working again, then gave him a little push upstream and let go. He rolled over belly-up at first. Just when I decided to grab him to use as fertilizer, he righted himself and became invisible against the dark bottom.

"Next time a trout," I said.

"I'll bet there are some big ones in here," said Caleb.

"You know there are," I said.

We liberated the remaining earthworms into a clump of ferns and replaced our hand lines in the pit under the grass thatch.

Caleb frowned. "Without the tubes in the pit, you can see there is an indentation. Somebody might poke around in there."

"We'll be back with the tubes before dark. We can arrange it then."

"I guess so," said Caleb. Possibly he had a presentiment that we would not return.

We placed the rubber tubes in the stream where the current was fastest, because we wanted to be whirled about. We lay across the top, rather than sitting in them: in places the stream was only six or eight inches deep.

It is a pleasure to stare at the sky and be bounced from one bank to the other, having no control over whether you move straight downstream or in circles.

"Look! That cloud is upside down!" said Caleb. I laughed and laughed at this, though I don't know why.

In fifteen minutes we heard the rushing of the little falls that dumped the stream into a backwater of the east branch of the Swift. This stretch of water was a dead end, cut off from the main river by a collapsed railroad trestle at its mouth. It plunged southeast for about a mile, swung past a rocky ridge called Dog Island, and disappeared into Cedar Swamp. If you paddled all the way through Cedar Swamp, you could get to firm enough ground so you could make your way back to the Palmer Road. That was a hike of over two miles. The backwater was yellow-brown, silted in, and could not have held a fish of any description. We were in this for the ride only.

Caleb and I got scrapes on our legs and bottoms as we were going over the falls. We paid no attention. We knew we would be in the water for at least the next hour.

There was a circular eddy in the big pool at the foot of the falls, so we had to kick our way out in order to resume floating downstream. The river was wide enough now so we did not bounce off the bank, except for once on a curve. The tubes did not turn around so often as on the stream; we went down headfirst. We knew there were no rocks before Dog Island.

I smelled the smoke before I realized we had passed the gravel pit and were level with the island. I was within a few feet of the far bank. I was dozing off, my arms and legs flopped into the water and my face turned away from the island, when I heard the gun go off.

"I'm hit!" Caleb yelled. I swiveled in my inner tube. Neither Caleb nor his tube was anywhere to be seen. I was directly opposite the big dead oak. There was a considerable volume of smoke coming out of the top hole and the face of a man withdrawing from the second hole, drawing a pistol in after him. The pistol began to reemerge just as Caleb's head popped up between me and the shore.

"He shot my tube!" said Caleb, spitting out water. "It's old Mullally!"

As the gun began to level off and the face to reappear, I slipped off my raft like a turtle off a log and dove as deep as I could. I imagine Caleb dove as well, for there was no second shot. I held my breath and kicked with the current for at least a minute, and came up south of Dog Island. Caleb was already on the surface.

"Go down again!" he said. "He might come running."

I needed no further encouragement to dive, and dive again, though my breath gave out more quickly than usual. I screamed and swallowed water when something bumped against the back of my head, but it was only my inner tube, which had kept pace with us. Dog Island was now out of sight. Caleb and I held the tube and lay on our backs until we were carried up onto the muddy beach at the bottom of the backwater. Here we lay for several minutes, easy targets. I felt I could not move a muscle.

Caleb rolled onto his side. "He's got a forge or something there," he said. "I could smell metal or iron. It was like the blacksmith's shop."

"In a tree?" I said.

"Probably needs to be by himself, apart from the sheriff and the law," said Caleb.

"I always thought it would be the kindest thing for everybody if he could be off by himself," I said.

"He's crazier than a bug," said Caleb. "Now we have to tell the sheriff. I don't know if he was aiming at me or the rubber tire, but I don't think he is that good a shot."

"I'm sure he didn't know it was us," I said. I was thinking of Pudge.

We struck out overland and by midafternoon were back on the Palmer Road. Instead of turning north toward the mud pond, we cut south and took a path that led around the flank of Mount Healy, then north back to the farm in Enfield.

We must have looked a sight as we trudged up the lane. Grandma dropped her book and said, "Where have you been? You look like something tried to eat you." I looked down and saw both of us were bleeding around the knee and calf. Grandma hurried inside to fetch a damp kitchen cloth. The cuts weren't much, though.

They never did bring a charge of attempted murder against old man Mullally, so Caleb and I didn't have to testify. When the sheriff's men went out to the island to investigate, they found him all set up with an illegal foundry, cooking away in the bottom of that old tree. He acted like he didn't think there was anything wrong with it, complained about his business being disturbed as they marched him off to the magistrate. Fortunately for him, he was able to spill the beans on some bigwigs in Athol and Gardner who acted as the fences for the coinage he produced, so he was allowed to plead guilty to operating the foundry and passing counterfeit coins. He eventually served fifteen months at the Worcester House of Correction. No one would hire Mrs. Mullally that year, even though she was a darn good science teacher. I don't know how they made it through 1938 and 1939. Maybe he had some buried treasure.

"What do you expect from a Harp?" was Uncle Ed's reaction to the whole business. "He's been two sandwiches short of a picnic since the day he was born."

———

———

IN early June the edge and quickness seeped out of the air. At first it was only a stillness, a stillness that bore promise of heat. By the time of the last Enfield town meeting, on the fifteenth of the month, the air had become hazy. The swarms of hornets were clouds in the treetops. It was possibly my imagination, because of the flooding getting nearer, but life in the Valley seemed off rhythm, unreal, as though seen through gauze.

Considerable excitement was occasioned by word that a radio station in Hartford, Connecticut, was going to send professional radio people to interview citizens of Enfield at the last town meeting. Sarah Pettingill, the postmistress of the town, purchased a new white dress from Hargraves's shop—the merchant's last sale, as he closed his doors that afternoon—so that she would look her best for the interview. Honus Hasby, on the other hand, declared that the radio crew had no business interfering in the deliberations of the town, that it was a private affair. His was the minority view. "Honus thinks all affairs are private," said Grandma.

The meeting was presided over by Uncle Ed as the town clerk. He seemed more ill at ease on account of the publicity and attention than I would have expected.

Sarah Pettingill asked to be recognized concerning an item of business not listed on the warrant for that evening. She stood in her place and addressed the chair in a voice somewhat louder than usual, clearly pleased with her new

———

dress and not unaware of the microphone in front of her.

"Mr. Chairman, my name is Sarah Pettingill, as you know, and I've had the honor to serve as the postmistress of the great town of Enfield for the last thirteen years. May I say, I am grateful to the citizens of Enfield for having reposed such a measure of trust and confidence in me, and I shall treasure every memory of our intercourse as neighbors."

Uncle Ed was staring at Miss Pettingill. "Do you have a motion you wish to make?" he asked.

Miss Pettingill glanced shyly to either side, as though to indicate that she would make no complaint concerning the boorishness of the question. Lifting her chin toward Uncle Ed, she said, "I meant to say only that I have such a wonderful feeling about this town and all the inhabitants here that I feel it would be appropriate for us to elect officers at this meeting to serve full three-year terms, as has always been our custom, or until such time as their successors shall be duly selected and qualified."

"Sarah, this town will be underwater in ninety days," said Uncle Ed. "Why do you want to have town officers presiding over the water in the Valley, when the town is not here?"

Miss Pettingill smiled understandingly, gave her head a little shake to the side, and said, "Oh, I know, I know. But, you never know!"

"That's right," said an old man in the back. There was a murmur of assent around the room.

So Miss Pettingill was elected to another three-year term, and so was Uncle Ed, and so were Clayton Hawley and Seth Quisenberry Jr. and Hamilton Darey. In the latter two cases, the terms outlived the incumbents, as Quisenberry was dead from scarlet fever and Darey hit by lightning while woodcock shooting before the reservoir was half full.

———

AFTER the business portion of the meeting, the crew from the radio station took their microphone around to folks in the hall. The long cord slithered like a snake behind them. The two men were dressed in fancy blue-and-white shirts, their sleeves rolled halfway up the forearm. Neither one had removed his hat. They had loose collars, and red neckties that did not reach down to their belts. Both of them had slicked hair and eyes constantly rolling back, like those of a fish on the surface of a pond. The fair-haired man seemed to have set out to model himself after his more seasoned colleague. They had an attractive young blond woman with them, with cascading curls under a smart beret, a beige sweater, and a tight navy blue skirt that stopped just at the knee. I believe it is the first time I ever saw a woman wearing a girdle underneath fancy clothes, and I must say the effect made a favorable impression on me. The woman spoke to people before they were interviewed, and made notes that she gave to the men. She seemed to be the only one who knew what she was doing. The function of the two men, apparently, was to make wise-cracks and snide remarks at the expense of whomever they were talking to at the time.

"Say, buddy," said the younger of the two to Homer

———

Putnam, who was fussing with his hat, "what do you say to your whole world being wiped out?"

"Oh, I don't think the stores could have sustained many more years here," said Putnam. "After the word got out, it was all downhill in the Valley, so at this point it's just as well." Lawyer Kincaid had sidled over to stand next to Homer and was nodding gravely.

"Surely you must feel some bitterness?" said the older radio man. Lawyer Kincaid took a step forward but Homer waved him off.

"Not at all," he said without energy. "They held hearings and observed the process. We all, each of us, received a letter from the government, saying that we had to be out by such and such a date."

"But why did you take that for an answer?"

Homer was nonplussed at this question. "Because," he said with emphasis, "we received a letter, from the government, informing us that we had to leave. That was it. That was the decision. It wasn't so hard to understand."

"But was it hard to accept?"

"I don't know what you mean by that, I'm sure. Understanding is accepting," said Homer, and went back to fidgeting about his hat.

Lawyer Kincaid raised a finger, indicating he would like to make another point, but the younger man ignored him. "How about you, sir, ma'am?" he said, moving on to old Dan and Mary Winship. "What's it like to have your world wiped out?"

The Winships were a favorite couple of mine in the town. Mary Winship would see me through her kitchen window, walking along the main street, and call out in a singsong, "Oh, Jamieson!" I would saunter indirectly over to her window, rather in the manner of a cat, making plain that I was not interrupting my important journey. She would say nothing, but there on the sill would be a plate with a delicious piece of white bread or toast, slathered with butter and strawberry jam. I would snatch it and take a wanton first bite, then try not to seem too much like a dog in gobbling down the rest. My payment for this treasure was to stand by the window while I ate, rather than running off, so that Mary might behold the consumption of her handiwork. There was seldom any conversation, but I could tell from her eyebrows that Mary Winship approved of me. She was also the only soul in Enfield who had ever spoken to me about my mother, and she spoke of her approvingly. That's all.

"Well, we don't really know," said Mary Winship.

"How is that?" said the young man, pressing his advantage. "How can you possibly not know what the future holds for you? It's your future!"

"We can't start again," she said simply. "We are realists, and we know we have to go."

"Where will you go?"

"Wherever they send us," she said, turning to Dan, who added, "That's right." He put his arm around her shoulder, defending her from the young fish half out of water.

The blond woman brought an end to this conversation by physically moving the cord and microphone across the hall to where the young folks were standing. She took the microphone herself for the first time and held it in front of Caleb Durand.

———

"What about you?" she began pleasantly. "What do you think about all this? Do you think it is the end of your world? Or do you think it is the beginning of something else?"

Caleb was taken with this, and of course with the woman as well. He stuck out his chest so that the microphone could hear. "I think it's the beginning of the grandest adventure I have ever known," he said. "The odd thing is we don't know exactly where it will all end. But it is an adventure nonetheless. The day of the flooding will be the first day of the rest of my life."

"And what about your life here, in the past?" continued the woman. "Has that been an adventure?"

Caleb frowned. "Of course it's an adventure, it's been an adventure," he said haltingly. "It's just that, we know it, we know our lives here. We don't know the future, and that's what is so exciting."

"And you have the government to thank for all that?" asked the woman.

"We have the government to thank," said Caleb.

———

At the end of the evening there was quite a bit of sniffling from the older ladies in the back rows. Lawyer Kincaid took over the lectern from Uncle Ed and made a declamation about how what is, is right, and folks must not pity themselves. He assured everybody that a better life awaited all of us because of the kindness of his fellow legislators in Boston.

Hammy stood up, right in front of Lawyer Kincaid, who seemed surprised to see him.

———

"I rise to a point of order," he said.

"You are out of order," said Lawyer Kincaid, bringing a gavel down. "The meeting is adjourned."

"I have something to say that concerns you. You cannot gavel me out of order."

"You have no fixed address. Persons with no fixed address cannot address town meeting."

"He lives in the Central Mass. locomotive, by the switching yard," said Wilbur Hodge.

"This goes beyond the scope of the warrant," said Lawyer Kincaid. "The warrant for the meeting is limited to the election of town officers and procedures relating to land taking and compensation."

"How do you know it doesn't relate, until you hear it?" said Hammy. A few of the farmers said, "Let him speak," "Let's hear what he has to say," and the like. I thought they were simply reluctant to have the meeting come to an end.

"I was taking a snooze in a boxcar at the switching yard yesterday afternoon, when I was woken up by raised voices," Hammy said to Kincaid. Now he turned to face the crowd in the hall.

"I looked through the slats. It was Lawyer Kincaid and that man Weller there from the Woodpecker crew. They were looking inside an envelope and arguing. Finally Lawyer Kincaid closed the envelope and took it." He turned back to Kincaid. "What was in the envelope?"

You never saw such a smile as came over Lawyer Kincaid's face. "I'm glad you reminded me, Hammy. I had almost forgotten. It was a draft of legislation I had asked one of Eustace's men to bring from the State House in Boston. I am

---

proposing to increase the compensation paid for farms in the Valley. I was questioning Eustace because I wanted to be sure everyone was provided for, everyone here. Isn't that right, Eustace?"

Eustace didn't appear happy about being the center of attention. He shifted his weight and looked off to the side. "Yes sir," he said. Lawyer Kincaid banged his gavel again.

Summer

D I R E C T L Y after the last Enfield town meeting, Lawyer Kincaid went back to Boston on an early train for the concluding session of the legislature. Quite a group gathered to see him off on the platform at Orange, including Wilbur Hodge and Homer Putnam, plus Grandma, David and Annie Richards, and others I didn't know. I noticed neither Hammy nor Eustace Weller was on hand, perhaps on account of the hour.

"Promise you will bring us results, Carl," said Grandma, pressing in his hand a "Prayer to the Great and General Court" signed by sixty farmers. He folded the document, slid it into an inside pocket of his black coat, and stepped forward to deliver his reply: "I am glad to have this document to deliver to the State House, and shall be honored to do so. I thank all who assisted in its preparation."

"Who are you going to give it to?" said Hodge.

Lawyer Kincaid coughed, looked at his watch, then at the huge farmer. "I shall deliver it—why, I shall deliver it where it will do the most good, of course. My aim is nothing less than to do everything that can be done. As it always is. I must get on the train."

"Carl, that train's not leaving until you say it is, and you know it," said Grandma. "Why don't you show us that piece of legislation that Eustace Weller brought you?"

Kincaid looked at Grandma. He fumbled at his coat pocket and mumbled something inaudible.

"You've got to stop the flooding, Lawyer, that's the one and only thing," said Hodge. "I know they've spent money on the dam already, but they waste money every day, and there's no sense throwing good money after bad."

Lawyer Kincaid nodded to the conductor, who pumped his arm. "All aboard!" I could not help feeling a thrill at the words. I must have shown it, as Lawyer Kincaid beamed at me and said with emphasis, "That's right, sonny!" He stepped lightly onto the moving step and removed his hat.

"You have my word, everybody!" he declared. There were a few shouts of encouragement from the crowd as the train picked up speed. I was not sure whether they were for the lawyer or for the train. Grandma was shaking her head.

"How does he do that?" she said to Sheriff Richards. "The farmers are grateful to him while he takes away their fields."

"It's a talent," said the sheriff, "though I'm not sure it's a

God-given talent. I think you have to work at it. Early and often, as they say."

"What do they say?"

"Vote early and often for Curley."

"Oh. Well, at least that rhymes."

"I wish I could be sure that Carl is doing everything he can in Boston," said the sheriff. "I keep thinking about the envelope that Hammy saw. I know what envelopes are for, on construction projects. I discussed it with the district attorney. He told me to come back when I could tell him what was inside the envelope. The 'alleged' envelope, he said. Said last time he checked, envelopes were commonly used for mailing letters and other communications."

"I must say, my first reaction was that Carl Kincaid would be too slick to do such a thing in the open," said Grandma. "But I suppose if a snake can sun himself in broad daylight, Carl can ply his trade there too."

———

As the days lengthened and the streams ran warmer, I decided I had had enough of civic events. If "reality" was the public celebration of past and impending deaths and destruction—which was what I now thought of organized town ceremonies—then I would let others deal with reality. For me, there was plenty of current to life in the here and now.

Summer was the season of the year when I was freest to be a boy. Caleb and I, and Potter and Will and Pudge, went without shoes; played endless games of hide-and-seek in the

———

hayloft, spreading hay over the climbing holes in hopes of luring others into a ten-foot fall; used the mounds and sandy trails of fire ants to replicate the armies of Antony, Octavian, and Caesar—though the inevitable kerosene-fueled blaze probably exceeded the actual horrors of antiquity; trapped bats in jelly jars at dusk, covering the mouth with cloth or perforated tinfoil so we could inspect their entirely human faces at our leisure; floated armadas of plywood and cardboard out onto the pond, to see them succumb, time and again, to bursts of powder and flame from deep within their holds. Cherry bombs in those days had fuses of up to five minutes, so the suspense was unbearable.

I kept an old Grumman aluminum canoe chained to an oak in dense brush by the south end of Darey Pond in Ripton. You couldn't get to it by land without going in up to your knees, and you needed shoes and long pants because the bushes were sharp. No one ever "borrowed" it, even though the chain could easily have been smashed. I don't know that anyone ever came across it. There was space in the Valley in those days, room to move.

One afternoon in late June, Hannah and I were discussing subterranean worlds, lost civilizations, fortresses that could never be taken, and treasures that could never be found. I managed to turn the conversation to my Grumman canoe. Hannah was immediately interested.

"Is it there now?" she said.

"Of course it's there now. It's always there."

"Let's go." She made no preparations, didn't put an apple in a pack, didn't check her footwear, just stood up. She was ready.

"We'll need paddles."

"You have a canoe, I assume you have paddles. Let's go."

She was right, I did have paddles. We stopped by the tool-shed, where I picked up an axe and a three-foot gaff—a pole with an iron hook at the end. They use it in handling tuna and other big creatures in saltwater fishing. I took the pine paddle and gave Hannah the ash, and we were off to Darey Pond.

I unlocked the Grumman, righted it, and threw the chain into the bow. Never can tell when you might find a better hiding place. Hannah held the stern. We skimmed our craft along the tops of the berry bushes, out to the mudflats at the pond's edge. Here we jumped into the canoe and poled ourselves along. I well knew who likes to lie in that mud, but I explained nothing, nor did Hannah inquire.

A flat-bottom canoe will move in three inches of water. Our destination was a depth of between two and three feet, which described most of the south cove of Darey Pond, once you were a few feet offshore.

I held the gaff, not my paddle, as Hannah guided us slowly over murky water. The middle of the cove was beginning to be choked with lily pads. We stuck close to the edge, where the water held either thin grasses or no weeds at all. A rotting wood-duck box on a post at the end of the cove stood as a re-minder that turtles ruled this part of the pond: no chick raised in that nest had survived to adulthood in my lifetime. Whoever had put the box up no longer maintained it. I sup-posed it was self-defense: you allow your heart to be broken only so many times, even in small matters.

I kept my eyes trained on the surface a few feet in front of the prow. Any further than that and you can't see the greasy bubbles. We made a circumference of the cove without spotting anything.

"Over there to the east?" said Hannah. She apparently did not need to be told what the gaff was for.

"Take her again," I said. "South is always better. Especially early in the season like this."

"You're the boss." She grunted with the effort of turning the canoe for another tour.

I felt the thrill even before I knew why I was excited. It's the same as when your hand finds the eggs in the top stall of the chicken coop. "Right there," I said. Hannah backwatered and the canoe stopped.

I pointed with the gaff to a patch of oily white foam, five feet in front of us, already dissipating on the surface. Hannah nodded and nudged the bow of the canoe forward to the left. She seemed to know it would be easier for me to pull up from the right.

"Looks like it's drifted a little," she said. "Try behind it."

I poked the gaff to the bottom, hitting mud and sticks. The water was almost four feet deep here, so I had to hold the gaff underwater to reach the bottom.

On my third poling, something seemed to grab the end of the gaff. I nearly let it go, but gave one last yank and it broke free, carrying nothing more to the surface than a mess of weeds.

We had drifted past the foam now, so Hannah circled back, taking care not to dip her paddle more than a few inches into the water. I was poking down every few feet, without much hope, when the hook struck something hard. I leaned over to maintain contact and almost capsized the canoe, as we were still moving. Hannah churned back, putting me directly above my quarry.

I pressed down, to keep him in the mud, and moved the gaff around to discover the edge of the shell, When the gaff slipped down, I pressed it deeper into the mud, then pulled back and up.

When I have engaged a snapping turtle in this manner, I move to get my hands out of the water as quickly as possible. On this occasion the gaff seemed stuck at the bottom, as though the turtle were tethered to a stump.

"I can't move him," I said. "I'm going to drop the gaff."

"Just hold on, we'll drag him," said Hannah. She tried paddling us into shallower water, but the canoe wouldn't move. It was as though we were anchored to a cinder block.

"Push with your paddle," she said. I dared not take a hand off the gaff, but managed to fix my paddle under my armpit and leaned into it. With Hannah also pushing, we dislodged the turtle from the mud and maneuvered the canoe into shallower water, where I had better leverage with the gaff—and both hands above the surface. We poled the canoe to a sandy spot just offshore, where bluegills made their nests. We beached it and stepped directly onto gravel in two inches of water. Now we could see that I had gaffed the snapper in the cartilage to the left of his neck.

He was thirty-five or forty pounds, and none too happy to have been roused from his nap. All four legs were clawing the air. His head darted and swiveled around, pure leathery evil. I pulled him onto the ground upside down, not wanting him to secure purchase.

Hannah grabbed a large stick and held it in front of the turtle's head. Not large enough: his jaws snapped it in two.

"Use your paddle," I said.

"But you gave me the good one. Don't you want to use yours?"

"You use it, I'm holding him down."

She held the handle of my paddle in front of the monster. The head darted out again, and for a second I thought he had bitten my paddle in half. The cracking sound was the paddle hitting his shell, as he tried to draw his head back in.

"Stand back," I said. I knew we had nothing further to fear from the jaws, as a snapper will never let go of anything he has bitten, but I was wary of the claws.

I planted my feet and held the axe at high noon. I waited for the turtle to extend his head, then hit him where the shell met the neck. In three strokes I had the head severed. The legs and claws were still working, and the head clung ferociously to my paddle. Hannah was holding the body down with the gaff, but her eyes were studying the head.

"How are you going to get that off?" she finally asked.

"Leave it there," I said.

After an hour the legs had stopped their convulsions, so we rolled the turtle's carcass into a sand pit and buried it as best we could. On the way home I made Hannah carry everything except the ash paddle and its insignia, which I held before me like a standard, hoping to encounter someone on the road.

On our return, I wedged the paddle into a snowplow hanging on the wall of the barn, where I hoped the rats wouldn't get at the head too quickly. Hannah and Grandma went to visit the turtle's head at least twice a day. Grandma said it was a lesson in tenacity. When the head let go and fell off after a month, the two of them buried it, and wouldn't tell me where. I don't know why women like to keep a secret. Maybe it goes back to the Virgin Mary, storing up things in her heart.

———

T H E next day Hannah told me she had seen Kathleen Connley and Billy Stark the previous night, dancing in the ballroom of the mansion by the lake in Prescott.

"I don't know them," I said.

"Kathleen and Billy were lovers at the time of the Civil War. Billy got back from the army and was building them a house by the lake. He was axe-murdered at the construction site a week before their wedding. Kathleen walked around in a daze for a few weeks. The doctors could find nothing wrong with her. 'I'm going to join Billy,' she told her father. 'Nonsense, dear, get a good night's sleep,' he said. She was found drowned in the shallow end of the lake the next morning, still in her nightshirt, aged nineteen years."

I thought perhaps the axe that felled the turtle had produced Hannah's reverie, but I kept this to myself. All I said to Hannah was, "How could she have died in the shallow end of that lake? It's only three feet deep."

"Maybe it has silted in some. Anyway, drowning is just an attitude. You can swim on top of a lake a hundred feet deep if you want to, or you can drown in two feet of water."

"Why wouldn't she just have stood up?"

"Maybe she didn't want to."

———

"Well, lucky you, you have five years left," I said. It was a rough joke, perhaps, but there's nothing I wouldn't have said to Hannah. I didn't know how much of what she told me was true, how much a dream, and how much imagination, and I didn't really care. She laughed.

I touched her shoulder. "Can you feel everything Kathleen felt?" I said.

She nodded. "That's the bad part. I can feel the love, but also the loss. I dreamed about them when I got home. I screamed in my sleep and woke up Jimmy Toolbox down the hall."

"He's not a good one to wake up in the middle of the night. Didn't he kill a man once?"

"Yes, but I've gotten to know him. He's hurt, more than anything. He couldn't kill a bluebottle if you gave him a fly-swatter."

"It's this power you have over people. I hope you don't take the stuffing out of me."

"I'm not worried about you. You'll always want to kill fish."

"I think that's true enough," I said.

———

Doc Crocker stopped by our house one morning after breakfast. He declined food and coffee.

"This is a business call," he said. "Lawyer Kincaid is back from the legislature, and is putting out the word that he's gotten a truckful of money for all of us. Says he's going to have an 'information' meeting in Enfield Town Hall tomorrow, to show us the schedules about who gets what."

———

"How much are we getting?" I asked.

"Whatever it is, we're not taking it," said Grandma. "Those boys in Boston will try to bulldoze the people, just like the buildings. They'll squeeze us so we won't be able to afford a farm in Pelham or Brookfield; we'll all wind up in tenement houses in Athol or Gardner."

"Might be nice to move to a big building in Worcester," said Doc Crocker, smiling.

"Bill, you know we need the land. I need the land, you need the land, we all need the land, or we wouldn't be who we are. They're taking away our land, and they damn well have an obligation to replace it."

"You tell them, Miz Hardiman. I'll hide behind you at the meeting."

The hall was packed the next day. Lawyer Kincaid gave a speech intimating he was letting us in on a big secret, a secret that worked to our advantage. He had worked hard in the legislature, he said, and had gotten a wonderful result. But this had to be it. He had exhausted the patience of his colleagues in Boston, and of the governor. If anyone complained or stood in the way, the deal would be off. This was take it or leave it. He distributed written schedules, showing what each landowner was to receive. I saw the sheet with the figure for our farm. It was a substantial sum, more than I would have thought our land was worth.

Grandma was at her most ferocious. She had been sitting at a school desk, and slammed the flat of it with her hand as she stood up. "Carl, you know that absolutely is not true," she said. "There are laws about the government taking private land. We have to get full value. This says Wilbur Hodge is getting two hundred seventy-five dollars. Wilbur Hodge has a hundred-forty-acre farm. How's he going to get that in Belchertown or Ware or Palmer for two hundred seventy-five dollars?"

If Lawyer Kincaid did not appreciate being addressed by his first name, he didn't show it. He bowed respectfully toward Grandma.

"Mrs. Hardiman, of course I'm entirely sympathetic toward what you say. It's just that there's a question whether anyone would pay Wilbur more than two hundred seventy-five dollars for his farm. If that's all anyone would pay, that's all the law requires the government to pay."

"But it's because you've said you're going to flood the Valley that no one will pay him for his farm," said Grandma, pointing a finger at Hodge. "They would have paid thousands if the legislature had left us alone."

"I note that the value for your farm is fixed at two thousand dollars, owing to its fine location," said Lawyer Kincaid. "The legislature has gone about the valuation process in a conscientious manner."

This statement was not relevant to the point Grandma had made, but it caused heads to turn. Whispers of "Two thousand!" could be heard. People looked at Grandma skeptically.

"Carl, I didn't write that schedule. For all I know, you're trying to divide us. All I'm saying is most of these values are depressed because of the announcement of the flooding."

"Mrs. Hardiman, I never said I was going to flood anything. This is bigger than any of us. Values go up and values go down. All the law requires is that the government match present value. What you have before you is not merely a fair disposition. It is the only disposition to which the appropriating authority will agree. It would be a pity if the applecart were upset, if you take my meaning. There might be no apples left."

Wilbur Hodge fidgeted with his hat. "I can't take nothing," he said. "Maybe we can find a farm at that price if we look further west, toward New York."

"That's thinking constructively, Wilbur," said Lawyer Kincaid. "Maybe we can even help you with that farm." He winked.

"I guess this is the best we can do," said Hodge. "Still, I'll miss the Valley."

Lawyer Kincaid got in the last word: "We all will, Wilbur. We all will."

————

WE were living parallel lives that summer, going about our regular chores and amusements while at the same time wondering what would come after the flooding. I wasn't worried about Grandma and me, but the more I learned about other families, the more I saw the hurt that was to come. They were simple people, accustomed to hard physical work but without any instinct for confrontation. When Grandma and Doc Crocker and Sheriff Richards suggested organized opposition to the proposed compensation awards, the farmers didn't want to hear about it.

Grandma was vexed by their passivity. "They're not fighting back, because they want to go on with their normal lives,

————

but this is going to destroy their normal lives," she said.

I must say, I have seen calves and pigs bow their heads before the axe. Grandma was more along the lines of snapping turtles, I concluded: offer no help to your executioner. No wonder she had so admired the turtle's head on the ash paddle. Perhaps she and Hannah had buried it in order to possess it.

———

THERE were, to be sure, further distractions from the Valley's political drama that summer. For me, most of them lived underwater. My favorite warm-water fishing was to trap a sucker or a shiner, thread a hook behind his dorsal so he could swim free, and send him to the bottom of one of the larger ponds from a raft. When you're catching crawdads or frogs for bass, or suckers or shiners for trout, the pursuit of the bait is often more exciting than the battle with the chief prey. It's a question of anticipation, and the teeming populations at the lower end of the food chain mean you are guaranteed success—noisy, splashy success. A wire basket with a sourdough roll in it seldom failed to produce forty hysterical minnows, salamanders, small catfish, and freshwater crayfish. The day seemed crowned with victory before the first line was cast.

The water had to be fifteen or twenty feet deep for this stratagem to work, and you needed a lead sinker to keep your minnow near the floor, but when all went according to plan it was a marvelous thing: a large trout or bass, scouring the bottom for freshwater mussels or crawdads, would be delighted to en-

———

counter a plump ready-to-eat minnow, squarely in harm's way and seemingly too confused to race away. The big fish would seize the smaller by the head, shake him a couple of times, edge a few feet away from his schoolmates so as to avoid detection, and then slurp down the whole mess, hook and all. You had to be patient and let out line at the first few yanks, rather than strike, so the big fish would not feel the line. Then, when he began his run with the prey tucked in his gullet, you would yarn him—strike strongly—and all hell would break loose. More than once we were toppled from our wooden rafts, in Goose Pond or Stump Pond, in fighting what turned out to be an eight- or ten-pounder.

The largest fish we ever caught in this manner was a thirteen-pound catfish, which made off with a sucker over ten inches long, just at dark, in late June of 1938. Roger Petty had the line, I had the net; Caleb and Hannah and Will Grain were watching from the shore. The fish refused to budge from the bottom for an hour and there was nothing for Roger to do. When it was almost pitch-black, the fish allowed himself to be maneuvered into shallow water, where Will Grain fell on him with a straight knife, driving it down through the flat of his head. The catfish broke free of the line at this juncture but was landed when Will, still holding the knife handle, put his other arm under the fish and heaved him onto the mudflat. Will screamed in pain and raced out of the water to roll around on the grass, so we thought he had cut himself. But the knife was still deep in the head of the catfish. The problem was the fish had stung Will's left arm with its horns, which were inches long and strong as a cattle prod. Will didn't stop moaning all evening, and bore the welts for a week.

———

Catfish are ugly creatures. This one had front ventral fins so strong it could raise itself up off the muddy ground in an effort to sting yet another of its tormentors. It put me in mind of Hannah's tale of having seen a phalanx of catfish walking across a narrow field, at night, down below the dam on Egypt Brook. She was met with ridicule at the time, but in biology class, Mrs. Mullally said some catfish really do walk on the earth; they have front fins almost like legs and that's how they get from pond to pond when one is drying up. I didn't know what to believe, but I had never heard Mrs. Mullally make a joke. Hannah took this small triumph without grace, hooking her thumbs into her ears and sticking out her tongue at whoever would look. The kids stopped ribbing her, but no one said she was right after all. The mystery of walking catfish may be one of the reasons I went into teaching biology.

———

THAT week Grandma found a nestling crow on the ground, with a broken wing, and nursed him back to health with milk and bread and a makeshift splint. For a time after he was restored to strength, he would not leave her shoulder. After that she persuaded him to take up a perch in the sycamore in front of the house, but he began to caw anxiously if Grandma disappeared from sight.

In a month he took up residence again with his brothers and sisters, but for the rest of the summer, if Grandma presented herself in the clearing in front of our house in the late afternoon, a single crow would shoot from the woods, as

———

though propelled by a catapult, straight to her outstretched arm.

Grandma was quite undone by this, though she would not say so. "He must be watching for me, every afternoon," was all she said. "That's after he's gone about his day's business," she added, lifting her chin, lest we think her grateful pupil lacked a full-time job.

Grandma was never sorry for herself. As much as she fought against the taking, she took her own advice never to complain. The only show of sorrow I saw from her in 1938 came one evening as she stood on the porch staring at the outline of the ridge. The talk at dinner had been of the imminence of our departure, and whether we would try to find the same type of farm close by the reservoir or move farther west, for more land.

"Who will take care of Mr. Crow?" was all she said. She bit her lip, but that didn't stop the tears.

I was fifteen years old, and I had come full circle on crows.

——

ONE of the jobs the Water Supply Commission gave to Governor Curley's Woodpeckers was to dig up and transplant every body in the graveyards of all five towns and eight hamlets to the new Quabbin Park Cemetery in Ware, on a nice spot of elevated ground. They found a lot more dead than there were stones or names attached to them—because there were many illegitimate in the Valley with no record of them, is what Grandma said. Not all babies, either: adolescents and grown men and women with no record whatever.

——

More even than lived at the poor farms in their heyday.

The graves of Captain Shays's rebels were all moved, but unaccountably were not grouped together at the new cemetery. I considered this an unforgivable violation of history, particularly for military men accustomed to formations. Even worse, the Woodpeckers came up one body short when they did the count on Shays's troops. Hannah said she supposed it was Henry Gruening. She remembered having known him as a girl, after she was Oriel Twynham but before she was Kathleen Connley. He had been shot in the back by Lincoln's men and lived for several hours, moaning that he was not ready to die.

"Didn't you have any happy lives?" I asked her.

"They were all full lives," she said. "I wouldn't have them any other way."

"What good does misery do?"

"It extends you, vertically and horizontally."

Of course Curley's men completely missed the Indian graveyards, the shallow ones, because they weren't marked. So when the hurricane came through the bare valley in September, it tore up a lot of skeletons that lay just under the surface of the land. Grandma was wild about this. Uncle Ed told her to relax. "Nothing to worry about," he said. "They've taken all the scalps they can."

Even the regular graves were dug only to four feet a hundred years ago, not six feet as today. If they were anywhere near the roots of a big tree or stump, the tree and the roots got plucked up by the hurricane, and there would be the body, a-moldering but abroad upon the land once again. The wind pinned a dead man to an oak tree in Enfield in a standing position, like he was just leaning on the tree to have a smoke. That was the picture that Doc Crocker took, the one I have on my dresser.

———

As the heat of June settled into the land and the Woodpeckers acted even more like an occupying army, the normal civility of Valley folk began to give way. There was a row at the Enfield church when the sexton found a brick with the number 666 baked into it, left on the floor of the pulpit so that Moncrieff would have stubbed his toe on it if it had not been found. People were talking in the pews before services started. Henry Houlihan leaned into our pew and whispered something urgent. I caught the words "handfasting," "fairs" or "Thayer's," and "moon." I asked Grandma what handfasting meant and was told to mind my own business.

I knew the full moon would coincide with Midsummer's Eve, that coming Thursday. At supper on Thursday I detected an edge of anticipation in Grandma, but affected not to notice it. I read *The Golden Bough* by the fire for a while after supper, then excused myself early to bed. In an hour I was awakened by the arrival of guests. Evidently they had not come to socialize, as there were no audible greetings. Everyone kept their voices down. I lay motionless so as to miss as little as possible of the conversation below.

"You must be careful," said a voice. I thought it might be Gene Gilroy, who had a bit of a Canuck lilt. "Leaving the brick in the pulpit was folly. People know what that number

———

means. Moncrieff may not have a majority, but I'd not like to see the reinforcements he could draw from the east if the lines are publicly drawn."

"Shays all over again," Grandma said. "But to shut it down would be unthinkable defeat. We would be laying down our lives trying to appease their morbid God, once again."

"We agree," said a third voice. "It's not worth discussing."

At that point there was silence. I feared I might have caused a floorboard to creak by shifting in my bed. I heard the front door shut, but did not move.

It grew dark at half past nine. At a quarter past ten I could stand it no longer. I dared not creep down the back stairs—they made more noise than a red squirrel in the woods—so I slipped out the window and down the grape trellis, dividing my weight between the slats and the vines. As soon as I hit the ground I moved flush up against the house, so as not to be seen from a window. Not a sound from within.

I bent double and moved quickly till I was out of the clearing, then put a thick maple between me and the house and straightened up to take my bearings. Thayer's Wood lay a little over two miles away, just over the Ripton line and about a mile from the ruins of the church. I avoided known paths that might be used by others, and stuck to game trails and streambeds. Given the clear sky and the full moon, this was not difficult work; indeed, I wished I had exchanged my light checked shirt for something darker.

Just before Thayer's wood there is a half-acre meadow on high ground, framed on the east by birch, on the west by a stand of oaks, to the south by a magnificent old orchard gone to seed, and by the wood to the north. I was picking my way through the orchard, moving from tree to tree, when I saw a light approaching through the wood from the direction of Ripton Centre. I knew of a large apple, at the edge of the meadow, that had been struck by lightning and was completely hollow below a hole at its joint. I raced over to it and plunged into the hole feetfirst, hoping not to trample a family of squirrels, or worse. My luck held, and I drew my head down to a foot below the opening. A knothole afforded me a three-quarters view of the meadow. The tree's branches stretched up another dozen feet after the hole in the trunk, so I had some comfort that my hiding place would blend with its fellows.

The light proved to be a torch, held aloft by a man and a woman dressed in full-length white robes, leading a procession of twenty persons, men and women. The men were naked to the waist and wearing skirts of some rough material I could not make out. Their shoulders and chests, when the light fell on them, glistened with a dark bath or moisture. Some of the men carried jugs, a few of the women loaves of bread. All of the participants seemed intoxicated or at least excited. I thought I saw the face of Gene Gilroy in the crowd.

The woman and man in white robes faced each other in the center of the clearing, as though to dance. Instead they touched their bodies to each other, the man saying, "Toe to toe, knee to knee, heart to heart, fist to fist, head to head."

The man held the torch in his right hand and a five-pointed star in his left. I have seen that star before, I thought. The woman held a wand in her left hand and a curved knife in her right. I had seen the dagger before, in fact I had held it. The woman passed it through the flame five times, then ran to the edge of the clearing and around its perimeter, dragging the point of the knife in the grass behind her. They must know I am here, I thought. I looked for Hannah in the crowd but she was not among them.

Several of the followers dipped torches of their own into the flame of the chief celebrant, then moved out to take up positions around the circle.

The man placed his hands on a bushel of corn that had been set before him in the middle of the clearing. His back was to the north woods, his eyes closed, his face shining. I had seen him at the Enfield town meeting.

"Goddess of good green earth and of the shining moon among the stars," he chanted, "goat-foot god of countryside and the wild woods, grant us understanding of the craft, wake the living dead among us, help us to find divinity in your kingdom and in ourselves."

"Teach us the wisdom of the druids and foresters, the miller's word and horseman's word," the woman said. Her face was painted green and white. "Teach us, goddess of the greenwood and of wild beasts, guide of the changing seasons, the life-affirming joy within us." The light fell on her high cheekbones and I knew her. She was the woman in the court-room, the woman in the bonnet.

"Grant that our fields, our livestock, and our bodies may be fertile," the man chanted, "that we may re-create your spirit, dying and reawakening." Change the words and he may as well be a priest offering communion, I thought. He poured a dark liquid onto the bushel of corn before him, at which point every torch in the meadow was extinguished at the same moment.

———

I heard movement around me, but not a human word. I was certain my trembling would shake the branches of my apple tree, leading to my discovery. After a time all noises died away, except for the beating in my chest and pounding in my temples. I stayed wedged in the tree until just before first light, then made my way back to the farmhouse. After removing the bark and twigs from my clothes and hair, I walked in the front door as though I had been out for a stroll. No one was about. I stole up to bed and slept like a stone.

———

T H E voice of Lawyer Kincaid rose from the porch to wake me hours later. I looked out the front window. I was sure he had come with a writ from the Ripton church fathers to exact retribution for the events of the night before, but his tone belied any such mission.

"The very top of the morning to you, Mrs. Hardiman. Might Mr. Hardiman be available on the premises?" He removed his broad-brimmed hat and held it before him, like a shield.

"He's here, if that's what you mean. In the kitchen. Said he was to meet you. Go on in and call for him."

Lawyer Kincaid demurred, so Grandma herself stepped onto the porch and yelled into the house: "Ed! It's the lawyer!"

At these words Lawyer Kincaid winced and clamped his hat back onto his head. It's strange how the life goes out of a person's eyes when they set their jaw, I thought.

———

There was a shuffling and a scuffling, a clomping on the two stairs down to the porch. Uncle Ed emerged blinking into the sunlight, tugging at the back of his suspenders to get them straight. I was put in mind of the rats we took out of the barn.

Uncle Ed was wearing a suit I had never seen before. Neither man said anything. Lawyer Kincaid jerked his head. They set off down the path to the little pond with the swamp adjacent, the lawyer walking straight and choosing his ground to avoid moisture on his shoes, Uncle Ed shambling along, still fiddling with the front of his suspenders. I lost them at the turn with the willow. I sensed movement in the woods behind them, off to the right, and thought it might be a deer. When I turned to look, it was Francis Perrault, moving from tree to tree.

"What's going on there, Grandma?"

"What do you think?"

"I don't know why they would want to meet here. It's not like we've got a special swamp, or Lawyer Kincaid likes to pick mushrooms or anything."

"Very good, Jamieson. No, I reckon Ed didn't want his neighbors seeing him meet the lawyer at his place. Ed's no fool, he knows Carl Kincaid is going to have to explain that envelope at some point."

"The one from Eustace Weller?"

"If you want to think that's who it's really from. Myself, I wouldn't have said Eustace was independently wealthy."

———

———

IN late June, Miss Ettie announced to me and Grandma that she was leaving the farm the next day and moving to Worcester. She was pleasant and matter-of-fact about it, but of course my mind was racing.

"Did we do something wrong?" I asked.

Ettie took my cheeks in her palms. "No, Jamieson Kooby, you didn't do anything wrong, you dear boy. You did everything just right. It's just that I'm an old lady, and in three months this farm is going to be underwater, and I have to look to my opportunities."

"Are you going to keep teaching at the school? I mean, at some school?"

She shook her head. "I've gotten a job at a clothing store, right on Mechanic Street. They sell all the latest things, so it should be easy to meet people."

"I'm all for you, Ettie," said Grandma. "I think this is just right. I only wish Jamieson and I were as well organized. We can't even decide whether to go east or west."

"East is closer to Boston, Miz Hardiman."

"You're right, of course we'll go west," said Grandma.

"Do they sell men's clothes, or just ladies'?" I asked.

"Just ladies', but if you visit, you can give me advice about the styles."

"I've got an eye for beauty," I said.

"I know that," said Ettie. She gave me a long kiss on the forehead and went up to her room to pack. My chest was pounding.

"This is a godsend for her," said Grandma.

"Why do you say that?"

———

"She can do better than Francis."

"Better than Francis? What did Francis do?"

"Oh, come on, Jamieson, you old rascal."

Wrapped as I was in the self-absorption of youth, I was without a clue.

———

T HERE was a ceremony on the first day of July to dedicate the cemetery in Ware as soon as the last bit of earth had been patted down. Many of the Woodpeckers were in attendance, some leaning on their shovels out of long habit. Pudge Mullally squirmed in his formal clothes.

"I can't believe it's Dedication Day again already," he said.

"That was Decoration Day, Pudge."

"What's the difference?"

I drew breath to explain, then hesitated. "You're right, there isn't any difference."

When the consecration was complete, Hannah went and stood right in front of Lawyer Kincaid, facing him. "Doesn't it trouble you," she said, "that they've had so much trouble accounting for the dead? People have been lost, and families have been split up."

"People have also been found, Miss Corkery. The population of the Valley is growing day by day. But in any event, from what I understand, these are your constituents, not mine. Even if they were my constituents, I can tell you that not a one of them has complained to me."

Hannah's eyes narrowed at Lawyer Kincaid's departing

———

back. "I think I know someone who might complain," she said.

"Who is that?" I said.

"A lady who has been wronged," said Hannah.

T H E next morning I was minding my own business, leaning against Hammy's locomotive and playing mumblety-peg
with a pocketknife, when a woman with long brown hair and
high cheekbones appeared at the edge of the birch stand. She
was holding up her skirts and picking her way between the
patches of mud. Hammy was propped up against the engine,
reading a book that Grandma had lent him. He bounced up
and greeted her, book in hand.

"Miss Millie, how be you this fine day? Can we be of
service?"

"I'm so sorry to trouble you. Hannah and Ettie told me I
must come."

"Not at all, not at all. Could my young man here fetch you
a spot of tea?" This was not a serious suggestion, but it was
taken as one. Perhaps Millie felt out of her element and did
not know what to make of things.

"No thank you, this is more business than pleasure."

The situation now had my full attention. Millie Tiverton,
wanton madam and pagan princess, making a business call?
This thought might have occurred to Hammy: he planted his
feet well apart and folded his arms in front of him, the picture of dignity and decorum—and resistance.

Millie to her credit blushed and began to stammer. "It's

just, you see, Hannah said you had spoken up at the town meeting about the Woodpeckers taking money, and that I should tell you the story."

"The story?"

She spoke rapidly. "The payoff happens every week at my house, at the house I maintain. Yes, the famous one."

"The payoff?" Hammy was not making it any easier for her.

"The contractors and engineers are making a fortune from the project. They are afraid people in the towns will rise up and stop it. So they are paying the leaders in the towns to speak in favor of it, or at least not oppose it. The general manager from Boston is at my place every Friday, and so is Eustace Weller, and that's where the money passes hands. Eustace is the go-between."

"Who does he go between?"

"He gives all the money to Kincaid. Kincaid gives some to a few of the town officials, and some to clergy, for the churches. The only one who will support it openly is Charles Moncrieff. He doesn't care, he's not from here. Lawyer Kincaid had to tell him not to lay it on too thick, said folks would get suspicious."

"I know one suspicious lady," I said.

"How do you know this?" asked Hammy.

"After the general manager leaves—he never goes upstairs, he meets Eustace in the back room—Eustace stays and drinks and drinks. And talks and talks."

"To whom?"

"To me and the girls."

"Does he go upstairs?"

"He does. That's where he talks the most."

"Why have you said nothing until now?"

"Who would believe us?"

"Who would believe *us*?" I replied.

"I think someone might believe us," said Hammy. "I think the sheriff might believe us. I'm quite sure he might believe us. In fact I think Judge Seabury might believe us."

"Hannah came to me and made me tell her," said Millie. "She said she knew something was going on and that I was involved, couldn't tell me how she knew. Said I must tell Hammy straightaway, he would know what to do. Ettie Clark, of course, has known for some time. She said Hannah was right, that I must come to you."

The thumping was in my chest. "How is it Miss Ettie has known for some time?"

Millie looked at me. "You're Jamieson, aren't you."

"Yes, ma'am."

"Well, she knew because I told her. Ettie is a person I confide in. We confide in each other."

"The top of the morning to you both," said Hammy. I knew what that meant. That meant clear out. I ran from the woods even before Millie, down the road toward Prescott.

———

T HE third of July, 1938, was stunningly hot, low-hanging air you felt you must push away from you in order to breathe. At a quarter past nine in the evening, at the hour between dog and wolf when it is impossible to see anything with or without a lantern, Hannah and I stood up to our necks in a muddy pool in the lower stretch of French King Brook.

———

Though we were totally immersed, it was too hot to move.

I was chewing on leek and wild onions from the field at the bank, thinking to confuse my tongue and thence my brain: sweet means hot, so sour must mean cool. No success: the mess ran putrid in my mouth. Out it went, making not a pretty sight on its way downstream. Hannah giggled, poking at the weeds and thinning spittle with a stick.

"So you've been giving legal advice to Millie Tiverton," I said.

"She's a fine person in an impossible situation," said Hannah. "But nothing will come of that courtroom proceeding. And nothing should. Sheriff Richards didn't know that Tommy Beckett was going to do the raid, or he would have stopped him."

"You're defending a disorderly house?"

"Certainly. I've often thought I'd like to work in such a place."

"As . . . ?"

"As anything. It would be like working at Conkey's Tavern. You see people at their most vulnerable. They can't give you speeches." She squinted at me to see how I was taking it.

"I have a horror of being lectured at, in case you didn't know," she said. I looked down dully, wrestling with the new perspective.

It was now quite dark at ground level, but I thought I saw Hannah stick out her tongue at me. I kicked her knee under the water and the moment was, thankfully, broken.

"Is that the real reason you went to see Millie Tiverton, to get a job?" I asked.

"No," she said. "I went because of some friends of mine."

———

We climbed out of the pool and lay on the bank.

"Why are you so in favor of vice?" I asked. "I've heard you defend drunkenness and tobacco, and now a disorderly house."

"Life is short already."

"Yes?"

"We might as well make it shorter. Look at that redtail way up yonder."

Sunlight had picked out the feathers of a hawk high overhead, bleaching it to albino. It was still daytime up there. We watched the hawk circle for a moment.

I wriggled over close to Hannah on my knees and elbows.

"You know they eat vermin and varmints," I said.

"I do know."

"Better watch out, then." I climbed directly on top of Hannah and lay there. "You can't be too careful, got to have cover."

She smiled and turned her head to the side.

———

THE next morning on awakening I thought I might be dead. There was no sound from anywhere. I moved my hand against the coverlet. Not a scratch. I tried to make a sound in my throat or swallow. Nothing came. There was no air in the house, no air in the Valley. It was five in the morning. There was nothing to do but close my eyes.

The day of the Fourth was an oven. All that was missing was a tin cover from Pomeroy to Zion to Mount L, and we would have been overcooked dishes for whatever gods were interested.

———

While we boycotted Washington's Birthday for reasons of local pride, none could outstrip us in enthusiasm for the Fourth of July holiday. The celebration was an excuse for hoses, fountains, sarsaparilla, and champagne: anything to cool off.

This was the day chosen for the visit to the field by the Honorable James Michael Curley. Lawyer Kincaid had announced that Curley would inspect the work of the Woodpeckers in the Valley through a visit to the old Swift River Hotel in Enfield. This was one of the few structures in the Valley that had been untouched by the Woodpeckers, since it was the headquarters for the Water Supply Commission. How even the governor was to accomplish this feat of inspection from a leather armchair in the library of the hotel had escaped me. Hannah said I was being overly technical.

"He's here to confirm the work, not to inspect it," she said.

"Why do they call it an inspection then?"

"To pretend they're doing something. It's like the king and his troops. All the work goes on beforehand. The buttons are polished, and so on. The king doesn't polish the buttons."

"You don't know anything," I said. This time I saw her stick out her tongue.

Grandma said everyone was to dress up regardless of their feelings for the governor or the project. In my case this meant that Grandma passed an iron over my shirt and trousers. I loved the smell of warm cotton. Caleb was not so fortunate, being cursed with the ownership of a pair of flannels, into which Missy Durand fastened him tongue and groove. He was like a man clapped in irons.

Governor Curley's private railcar arrived at a quarter past

two at the Orange station, where he was greeted by Lawyer Kincaid, other elected officials, and a large crowd. The governor, wearing a top hat, said a few words from the back railing of his car on the plight of the western farmer. He winced when Clayton Hawley asked if any in the crowd had a question. I suppose he knew his business, because the question, from a bright young woman, was this: "If you are intent on the well-being of the western farmer, why are you coming to Enfield to promote the flooding of five western farm towns?"

Lawyer Kincaid declared that after all there was no time for questions because of the governor's need to attend to pressing business. He jostled Curley into an open Packard, which at first failed to start. The crowd surged round the car. The governor and his attorney, both in starched collars, sat stone-faced and stared straight ahead at the road before them, as though the car was closed-top and they were traveling at a great rate. Their expressions relaxed only when the engine turned over.

At the Swift River Hotel, yellow bunting girdled all three buildings, including that reserved for the animals. Curley stood on the porch, his fingertips on the railing. He was a magnificent specimen of a man. The intelligence of his eye, the aristocracy of his brow and temple, were like blows upon the observer. Even before he opened his mouth, I would have done anything for him.

But Curley did not speak, at least not straightaway. He rasped a few words, then gave in to a fit of little coughs and pointed to his neck. "Throat . . . ," he whispered.

Lawyer Kincaid glared. "For pity's sake, fetch him a glass of water! Is there no water here?" he cried.

"There'll soon be plenty," said a voice from the back.

"Up, up for the mayor! Up, up for the governor!" piped a fat balding man in a morning coat, a diamond stickpin in his foulard and a carnation of Kelly green in his lapel. Curley smiled at the man and turned languidly to the crowd, as though to inspect his own reflection in a glass.

"I know many of you are troubled, I daresay all of us are troubled, about the impact that the flooding of the Valley will have on life as it has been lived here for generations, since the time of Captain Shays and before . . ." His voice was soft, conspiratorial. He was sharing a secret with us. There were no preliminaries, no "Laydees and gentlemun!" Nothing to suggest any distance between him and his audience. He and his audience were one. He was right, we *were* troubled, and he had put his finger on the cause. His rich voice gave assurance that he could make the trouble go away. I was comforted. He had mentioned Shays: he was talking to me!

"Nothing could be more precious than that life, nothing could or should ever be more highly valued than that life."

Hazel Knott elbowed her husband in the ribs. "He's right, you know," she said. The bill of his Ford Ferguson cap went up and down. It was the only time I saw the two of them agree on anything.

"We all of us are filled with an inchoate longing when we walk the lanes trod by our ancestors. We want to experience their lives as well as our own."

Yes, I said to myself. Yes, go on. Or stay here, linger on this point; either would be fine.

"In a sense, of course, we do so every time we stand in the shadow of a tree they planted, planted with us in mind. But the shade of the tree is not the essence we seek to recapture."

Every face in the crowd was turned up toward Curley, receptive, beseeching, drained of its own opinion and importance. Eustace Weller's mouth was open wide. He looked as though he had been hit with a stick.

"It is their spirit we seek to recapture, to distill and preserve so it may run through our own lives. It is the spirit of Captain Shays—" Here, I swear, he looked directly at me.

"The spirit of Captain Shays, who lived a full life in this Valley and yet saw instantly when circumstances required him to lay down the plow. He saw straight through to the end, knew when sacrifice was at hand, and stood his ground in the vanguard at Breed's Hill, at Concord and at Lexington." Curley was either a learned man or well briefed.

"Boldness was his temper, boldness the temper of his time." Curley stopped here, though it was clear he was in the midst of a thought. We could see the words forming in his throat. There was not a sound in the air, not a bird twittering. The silence made Curley the speaker more powerful. He used it. He was motionless, gazing intently at something just over our heads. Finally he drew a breath.

"It was a boldness that saw the future, that understood the balance between present sacrifice and later fruition. It was a boldness that asked nothing for itself, that merely took action, for the good of the whole."

The good of the whole. I had heard that before.

"Those acts," said Curley slowly, "have stood the test of time. They have worn well in the memory of men."

So far, so good.

"It is not given to every man and woman to perform such

deeds. Nor would we wish it. A life lived always at the center of a crucible would be leeched of pleasure."

Where is he going with this?

"Yet occasionally, perhaps once in a generation, the opportunity for a bold stroke is presented." He paused again, to let us process the thought. "Such an opportunity is upon us now.

"This is not a question of mine versus yours, friends, not a question of west versus east. This is a question of whether we shall act outside the confines of our antecedent lives, whether we shall plant a tree that we shall never see, whether we shall create the future through action, rather than through the mere passage of time."

"Now I understand," whispered Caleb. "Give me a sledgehammer so I can knock down my house. I want to create the future through action."

"Don't be disrespectful," I said.

"All of you gathered here are in the vanguard of action. I congratulate you, and I thank you so very much for your hospitality and your time and indulgence this day." There was strong applause from throughout the crowd. People like to be congratulated.

Curley was beginning to turn back toward his seat when a raised hand, and then a disorderly figure, appeared at the front of the crowd.

"Your Excellency and Your Honor, a small question?"

Curley had to know there might be rough water ahead, but given the manner of address, he could not cut his interlocutor short, no matter his shabby appearance. "Certainly!" he said.

"Why is it necessary," said Hammy, "for local sponsors of the project to be paid cash from the construction managers in Boston?"

"Not. Not at all necessary. Of course not!" The governor was smiling. Lawyer Kincaid was not. Curley caught his eye. Someone offered a toast. There was a general shout and cheer, and many a glass hoisted. Now both Curley and his attorney smiled.

———

IN the latter part of July, Honus Hasby left the poor farm in Prescott and moved to a fine house on a hill in Belchertown. How he had paid for it was anyone's guess. A number of the male boarders had been settled with relatives or moved at the state's expense. Only one man remained: a dimwit called Jimmy Toolbox because he could fix anything. He was a Pole who had been convicted of murder but released on a technical point of law. No one took the murder seriously because it occurred within a community where English was not spoken, so no effort was made to retry him. The local farmers would as soon have paid for the room and board of a fisher-cat who had killed a porcupine.

None of the female boarders had received any compensation from the commonwealth, as Lawyer Kincaid always referred to the government, so they were asleep in their beds when the crew of Woodpeckers arrived with their sledge-hammers at six in the morning. Hannah was already abroad; she had awakened before first light to find herself sitting on the swing by the big hickory, pumping high into the air. Once

———

awake she stayed there, holding on to the ropes, dozing and occasionally squinting at the outbuildings. At first, she said, she thought the Woodpeckers were bears. Then she realized they were too clumsy to be animals. They massed in silhouette about the springhouse, then the icehouse, then the main house, murmuring and pointing. The first sledgehammer was applied to the side of the house as dawn broke. Hannah simply stared as they went about their business and the occupants ran out the front door, clutching a box or a basket. Why there was not so much as a "halloo" was another mystery. Perhaps Curley's men felt the buildings had to be flattened so people would not be living above their station.

We heard about the razing of the poor farm from Roger Alcott, who had come by for some shoots and seedlings Grandma had promised him. "Paul Burlingame has them all at the police station and doesn't know what to do!" He laughed. Grandma received the news in silence. I knew she was thinking hard, because her head was stock-still. Normally her head would bob to and fro in conversation.

"There you be, then, Roger," she said, putting the produce in his hand. I was watching her immobile face as she waved good-bye to Roger and his sorrel. They were not even around the corner when the lines set next to her eyes.

Grandma went straightaway to the police station, me with her. "Polly," she said—that was the chief's nickname—"I don't know what your jurisdiction is over any of these people, but that poor girl Hannah is coming to stay with us or you are going to be regretful on account of past deeds, if you know what I mean."

The chief of police took off his hat and held it in his hands, more in penitence than defense. "Yes ma'am," he said.

So Hannah moved into Miss Ettie's room that afternoon. It had been vacant less than a month.

———

T H E first night Hannah spent in our house, there was a gibbous moon. I was awake when she slipped into my room. She had on a long white nightshirt. Her hair was down.

"I've seen Corporal Gruening," she whispered.

"Who is that?"

"The soldier whose body was missing when they moved the graveyards, the one from Captain Shays's regiment."

"Did you speak with him?"

"No."

"Were you walking outside just now?"

"No, I, I saw him in my room, standing by the door. He had brass buttons on his coat. He was looking for something. A place to rest, I suppose, poor thing."

Hannah was standing close to the head of my bed. I smelled the warmth of her body and judged she must have come directly from her bed.

"I want to put my hand around you," I said.

"Oh."

I put my hand against the small of her back, gently, and drew her toward me. As I did so she leaned over and stretched her hands before her, to avoid falling on the bed. This loosed her nightshirt, so that her chest was fully visible to me. I raised my head and took her breast in my mouth. I pulled her on top of me and ran my hands down her hips to

———

find the hem of her nightshirt. I drew it up slowly over her head.

"I want to get my hands on your back and my mouth on your front," I said.

I licked her stomach, licked the bottom of her chest, and ran my tongue back toward the left nipple. I set the edge of my teeth halfway up her breast, just at the point of tension but not, so far as I could judge, of pain. This was the sweetest flesh I had ever tasted, including fish and fowl.

Hannah closed her eyes, clasping my shoulders, drew in her breath, then let it out, saying, "Mmm." This caused me to harden and throb, and to sweat around my temples.

"Do you love me now?" she said. "I'm a girl and you're a boy after all, it appears."

"I've always loved you," I said. "I've loved you since you were a little girl. I didn't know you then, but I love the little girl you were. I can see her plainly. I love you as Kathleen Connley, as Oriel Twynham, and Henry Gruening's lover."

"Are you Billy and Samuel and the corporal?"

"No, but I can see you through their eyes." Her warmth made me giddy. I let myself go.

———

I had a powerful sense of well-being the next morning at breakfast. I did not speak with Hannah directly for fear my voice would crack. She wore a brown frock I had seen her wear a dozen times before, but the cloth was stretched across her front and I swear showed her nipples for the first time. There were other curves too, where I had never seen curves,

———

and a scent from her neck and arms where I had never noticed a scent. I did not exchange pleasantries with her, not under the razor-sharp eye of Grandma. I was in a high state, and grateful to get off on my own for my chores.

I went up to my room for my pocketknife before setting out for the day. You never know when you may need a knife, to cut a small sapling or a branch more neatly than you could break it. Or to whittle, or clean fish or game, or pare fruit, you never know. I kept my knife on the top of my dresser drawers, together with twenty-seven cents in change I had amassed. I could rely on these objects of hard metal to be there. The polish of the knife handle, the absence of any grain, contrasted with the oak of the dresser. One was taken from nature, the other visibly man-made.

I sat on the edge of my bed and stared at the knife and coins on my dresser top. These objects pleased me. They were the emblems of my independence as a boy.

I thought back to the previous evening, and ahead to the undefined future. I had surrendered myself, I was surrendering myself, I would surrender myself. I no longer had any doubt of Hannah's being Oriel Twynham, or Henry Gruening's lover, or Billy Stark's lover. Now she was my lover, and was to be my lover. She would tell the story of our love a hundred and two hundred years hence, to boys whose grandmothers and grandmothers' grandmothers had not yet been conceived. The boys, soon or late, would realize that they too would become the stuff of story. I closed my eyes and lay back, surrendering to my future.

I woke with a start and stood by the window, rubbing my eye. I was looking without seeing. A ghost stood in the yard

———

in front of me, a woman in a ball gown, a man on her arm in formal dress with a fancy white front. They were whirling and shimmering, as though underwater. I had fallen into Hannah's world.

I blinked. I had been staring across the low fence at the laundry line. The white dining room tablecloth had been hung to dry. The embroidery at its border, nearly touching the ground, had formed the hem of the woman's dress. The lace dresser top, hung next to it, was the white shirtfront of her gentleman companion. But I was sure I had seen the sway of hips at the top of the lovely white bustle.

———

AUGUST was the last month that the residents of the Swift River Valley would live together. You might have thought that would draw people closer to one another. Instead, it ruined every aspect of our communal life. Most of the wooded areas to be flooded had been cleared, a good number of the farmhouses leveled and carted off, and those who had found suitable property elsewhere had moved. The social fabric had already been torn; for whatever reason, people no longer seemed to take enjoyment in joint activities.

Some of the remaining families spent the month traveling through the western part of the state, as well as into southern New Hampshire and Vermont and northwest Connecticut, in search of land on which to resettle. Others, including Grandma, the sheriff, and Lawyer Kincaid, seemed determined to stay in place until the final deadline for demolition

———

in September. "Carl Kincaid is afraid what might happen in the towns if he leaves us alone, and he's right," said Grandma.

As the end of my world grew nearer and nearer, it seemed further and further away. My fishing expeditions were less frequent and less enjoyable; indeed, Potter and Will had already left. But this meant more time during the day with Hannah. And every night was with Hannah. I felt full. No change was threatening, particularly after Grandma made it plain she expected Hannah to move with us.

"Thank you very much, Mrs. Hardiman, you're very kind," said Hannah.

"You have marvelous manners, my child," said Grandma.

Thinking I could not improve on that exchange, I left them alone and walked out of the house to enjoy the day. We had only weeks left, but I found it impossible to think of the Woodpeckers or of Lawyer Kincaid. Perhaps Caleb had been right after all when he said a great adventure would begin on the day we left everything behind.

———

ONE morning at the end of August there was a pleasing foretaste of fall in the air. Ordinarily this would set me to thinking about acorns and slingshots; evidently it set Grandma to thinking about impending change. She was minding her cereal when suddenly she banged her spoon on the table, raised her head, and said, "You've got to go to Hammy."

"Why today? We saw him the day before yesterday," I said.

———

"He's not going to drive that engine to Orange or Athol, I can tell you that. Or even Ware. And he got no compensation from Carl's friends in the legislature, because they don't think he has a fixed address."

"I'd say his address is considerably more fixed than many in the Valley," said Hannah. "I'd like to see the Woodpeckers try to tear it down."

"It's not waterproof, though," said Grandma. "You've got to tell him he should move with us. He doesn't have to live in the house, wherever it is. He can have an outbuilding, or he might even like to build one. Or Jamieson, you could build one for him, all of logs, with holly and bay and viburnum in the chinks. He'd like that."

Within the hour Hannah and I were on the path to Hammy's engine. I was taking immense pleasure in framing the proposal in my head.

When we came to the last clearing it struck me something was out of place, though I could not say what it was.

"There's no smoke," said Hannah. "He usually has a fire at night and lets it burn down."

The first flicker of worry passed through me. "But it's been very warm," I said.

"Not last night. Or now."

We ran the last hundred yards, halloed without response, and looked inside. All of Hammy's things were there, even his books. Better if they had not been! Then he might have left on his own power.

When Hammy had not turned up in four days, Sheriff Richards announced he would conduct an investigation into Hammy's disappearance. Lawyer Kincaid told him he lacked the authority to do so, that only the district attorney, with the approval of the court, could empanel a grand jury to investigate in a case of this sort. The matter was brought before Judge Seabury, who ruled in favor of Lawyer Kincaid on the legal point. He summoned the district attorney to his courtroom.

District Attorney Fitzgibbons agreed with Lawyer Kincaid that a formal investigation of the disappearance of a transient vagabond would be a waste of resources. He and Lawyer Kincaid proceeded to the steps of the courthouse to explain their decision. Hannah and I stood in the front row.

"My job as your elected representative," said Lawyer Kincaid to the children and townspeople in the square, "is to prevent the waste of scarce resources."

"Like water," I heard myself say.

"Like taxpayers' money," said Kincaid.

"This is a matter of life and death!" said Hannah.

Lawyer Kincaid looked down. "We don't know that, miss," he said, "but we do know it's a matter of taxpayers' money, and it's a waste of that money."

Fall

At Winsor Dam, the last gravel fill was poured through the last filter into the last pit on Labor Day 1938. The Woodpeckers were none too happy about working that day, and raised a fuss all the way to Boston in order to be excused, but word came back from the governor that all had to be in readiness for the closing ceremony on September 21.

There had been a pile of wind and rain in the days leading up to the twenty-first, and reports that a storm had ravaged much of Long Island, in New York State, and battered Rhode Island. But the day broke mild and still, oddly still. There was not a cloud at 9 A.M., though the color of the sky did not seem right. The trees stood tall, straight, and motionless, like men facing a firing squad.

At half past nine, preparations were in full swing at the old Swift River Hotel, now the last outpost of the Water Supply Commission. Deviled eggs and cucumber sandwiches were set on card tables on the immaculate lawn that sloped gently down to the river. Every portico of the hotel was decorated with bunting—not the black crepe of the final ball at the Enfield Town Hall, but spanking red-white-and-blue. United States flags posted from every vertical beam of the porch crackled smartly as the breeze picked up during the morning.

At eleven o'clock, the long low black cars began pulling up to the back of the hotel, discharging their distinguished cargo onto the oyster-shell terrace. It must be true that society arrives late, as the last car to roll down the drive contained none other than I. J. Gielgud, chief of technical operations for the project, and Frank Winsor himself, the chief engineer, trim as a bandbox in full mustache and bowler.

By this time a crowd of a hundred people had gathered on the lawn below the porch. The ladies in charge of preparations, reassuring one another that the day was fine, were scanning the sky.

"At least there is no sign of rain," said a plump, enthusiastic woman. This was Betty Catlett, wife of the construction manager. She smoothed her apron with both hands, indicating a state of readiness for whatever lay ahead. She would be moving back to Boston with her husband within a week.

"I don't really care for the darkish color there to the south," said Hazel Knott. Hazel had already moved her family to Hopkinton, had returned for the day.

———

199

"That's not rain," said Betty.

Uncle Ed walked up to the two women. "What is it, then?" he asked. "Doesn't look normal."

The breeze had picked up to a point where the eggs and sandwiches seemed in peril.

"Why don't you all help yourselves to the food?" offered Hazel. "We'd hate to have these card tables tip over in the wi—in the breeze. Or whatever."

"Oh, no!" said Betty. "I promised Mr. Winsor no one would eat a thing until he had finished speaking."

"Eating deviled eggs don't make much noise," said Uncle Ed, popping one into his mouth. Hazel Knott took a stack of three cucumber sandwiches. Betty Catlett glared at her, then took two deviled eggs herself.

At that point there was a piping from some of the women standing nearest the back of the hotel. The wind had picked up oyster shells from the drive and driven them into the crowd.

"He better hurry up and talk," said Uncle Ed.

By now Winsor and Gielgud had made their way to the center of the front porch. Winsor stepped to the balustrade. The flags were taut as frozen sheets now, no longer flapping, and Winsor had to squint into the crowd. There was moisture at the outer edges of his eyes.

"Ladies and gentlemen—" he began. He's no Curley, I thought.

That was all anyone heard. With a crack more like that of a rifle than a shotgun, the big walnut tree behind the hotel snapped at its base and crashed down on the roof of the rear section, cutting through two stories as if they were papier-mâché.

The screaming began in earnest. The crowd on the lawn tried to scatter, but most of the motion was circular as there did not seem to be anyplace safe to go—certainly not into the hotel.

Clayton Hawley ran out the French doors of the big room behind where Winsor was standing.

"Evacuate the building! Evacuate the building!" he shouted.

Winsor and Gielgud looked uncertain. There was no way for them to evacuate the building without the substantial loss of dignity entailed by climbing over the porch and jumping down into the crowd. This, however, they were rapidly obliged to do, as shingles began flying off the porch roof like clay pigeons from a trap.

The crowd, seeing that the headquarters was far from a place of refuge, moved pell-mell down toward the flatland adjacent to the river. Two of the card tables that had been pressed into use for the picnic flew over our heads at a height of thirty feet. Even in those emergent circumstances, I could not help myself from thinking that they would have made an easy shot. My arms followed them.

Hazel Knott had thoughts of her own. "I'm glad at least we started on the food," she said to Betty Catlett, who was sobbing and stuffing a bandanna into her mouth.

"What will Mr. Winsor think?" she said. "Will he blame me?"

"No, dear, of course not," said Hazel.

Most of us were now lying prone on the ground, to avoid

being blown over. The wind was all out of the south. As there was no structure or tree behind us in that direction, I judged we were as safe as we could be. I turned to feast my eyes on the death struggle of the Water Supply Commission. Bits of wood and siding were shooting off like cinders flicked by an unseen finger. From inside there was a sound somewhere between a groan and a scream.

"Are people trapped in there?" I asked.

"No, son," said Doc Crocker. "She's just about to go."

The whole building seemed to stand on tiptoe for a moment. Then the remainder of the roof flew off in one piece, and the four walls collapsed like playing cards.

The hurricane of 1938 might have been surprised, on touching down in western Massachusetts, to find an entire river valley with only one magnificent structure standing in it, but it made short work of that structure. By one o'clock all that was left of the Water Supply Commission headquarters was the cellar hole. I raised a fist in triumph for Mother Nature.

———

Dᴜʀɪɴɢ the height of the hurricane the next day, you could smell the ocean in Enfield. The storm had moved from Rhode Island to the Swift River at a speed of seventy miles per hour; the saltwater scent was fresh.

In addition to playing havoc with the Indian graves, the hurricane tore up the trees at the edge of a swampy pool in Ripton, and there was the body of Hammy the hobo, bound to a railroad tie from the abandoned Central Mass. line. His head had been bludgeoned. The twine was the same the Woodpeckers had used in removing brush from the Valley.

With a body presented, Sheriff Richards needed no one's permission to conduct an investigation. Old Mrs. Hatcher, who lived in the last house before the edge of the woods, at the end of the road, said she had been puzzled to see Eustace Weller and two other Woodpeckers tramping down the lane inside the woods, carrying lumber, late in the day before Hammy had disappeared. She had not realized until questioned by the sheriff that the time matched Hammy's disappearance.

The two other men were arrested, but before the sheriff's men could find Eustace to take him, he rowed out to the middle of Darey Pond and jumped overboard. Neighbors heard him, but Eustace was drowned by the time they reached him.

"Couldn't swim a lick," said Uncle Ed. "And Ireland is surrounded by water."

I kept my own counsel, but I couldn't help thinking of Eustace's kindness to little Pudge Mullally. While he was big enough and strong enough, I couldn't believe he could beat a man to death.

———

In the Orange courthouse the next week, Lawyer Kincaid defended the two other Woodpeckers at the murder trial before Judge Seabury. Sheriff Richards was specially appointed to prosecute the case on behalf of the common-

———

wealth, and introduced the evidence from Mrs. Hatcher, who identified the men, and the twine, and a bloody stick of lumber that had been found. The defendants seemed scared and kept looking at Lawyer Kincaid. Lawyer Kincaid put the older man on the stand and asked whether it wasn't true that the two men had been attending an organizational meeting the afternoon Hammy was killed, and that Eustace Weller had been absent. The man assented. Lawyer Kincaid asked him who had been present at the meeting. The man seemed confused. Lawyer Kincaid leaned into his face and asked, "Don't you remember, sir, that I myself was present at the meeting?" The man said yes. Sheriff Richards jumped up and called for a mistrial and for Lawyer Kincaid to be discharged as counsel in the case. Judge Seabury agreed. He seemed angry with Lawyer Kincaid. The case was set down for trial again in two weeks. Lawyer Kincaid posted bail for the two men, out of his own pocket.

———

JUDGE Seabury was a busy man. Two days after the mistrial of the Woodpeckers, his courtroom was again standing room only, as the long-delayed charges against Millie Tiverton came up to be heard.

To the surprise of many including myself, Sheriff Richards had agreed to assume the conduct of this case for the commonwealth, as an accommodation to the district attorney. Evidently Mr. Fitzgibbons did not relish the prospect of a return engagement before Judge Seabury.

———

In the hands of David Richards, the government's evidence and the testimony of the police witnesses were considerably more restrained than in the previous session. At the conclusion of the prosecution's case Judge Seabury frowned at the sheriff.

"Is that all you have, sir?"

"That is all, if Your Honor please. The commonwealth is well content."

"Not much more than the last outing, Sheriff." The judge seemed troubled.

"The commonwealth is nonetheless well content, Your Honor."

"I see." The judge turned to Millie Tiverton's defense attorney, Oswald Adams, an able advocate—and friend and hunting partner of David Richards—who had remained rooted to his seat, his head down, throughout the presentation of the government's case.

"Mr. Adams, do you have a motion?"

"No, Your Honor, but the defense desires to present evidence."

"Do you not have a motion for a directed verdict of not guilty?"

"No motion at this time, Your Honor. Merely a witness."

"Very well, it's your funeral."

"I call the defendant to the stand, Your Honor."

This produced considerable hubbub among the veteran court watchers in the back rows.

"What's he doing?" asked one.

"Highly unorthodox," said another.

Millie Tiverton, duly sworn, gave her name, address, and general background information. She was blushing. Oswald Adams, polishing his spectacles, leaned a little closer to the witness stand.

"Do you maintain premises at Two Pilcher Road in Greenwich?" he asked.

Millie looked straight ahead. "Yes sir."

"And do you entertain there, both gentlemen and ladies?"

"I do."

"And serve beverages to the gentlemen, for which you charge a fee?"

"Yes."

"You are a licensed innkeeper, and the house has seen use as a tavern since the last century?"

"That is true."

"The ladies sometimes repair to the second story?"

"Sometimes."

"Have you ever been present in a room upstairs with any of the ladies in your house?"

"Never."

"Do you feel you have done anything wrong?"

Judge Seabury looked quickly at the sheriff when this question was put, but the sheriff sat still as a stone at his table, staring straight ahead.

"No objection, Mr. Richards?" said the judge.

"No objection, Your Honor."

"The question is surely objectionable," said the judge to both Adams and Richards.

"No objection," said the sheriff.

"May I answer, Your Honor?" said Millie Tiverton from the witness box.

"Very well," said Seabury.

"No, I do not feel I have done anything wrong," said Millie.

Oswald Adams sat down, prompting another murmur. "Your witness," he said to Richards.

Sheriff Richards rose in his place but did not advance an inch toward the witness.

"Did a man named Eustace Weller frequent your house?"

"Yes."

"And a man named Catlett, the construction manager for the flooding project?"

The judge interrupted. "What does this have to do with the price of tea in China?"

"This is cross-examination, Your Honor. The defendant is presumed to be hostile to the commonwealth. Massachusetts, as Your Honor knows, follows the wide-open rule on cross-examination."

"She does not appear excessively hostile."

"She is presumed to be hostile, Your Honor."

"Very well. No objection, Mr. Adams?"

"No objection, Your Honor."

The judge sat back, staring at the ceiling. "This is *my* courtroom," he said.

Millie smiled at him. "May I answer, Your Honor?"

"Yes, you may answer." He sagged forward onto his pulpit.

"I know Catlett." Her eyes narrowed. "He was the one who brought the envelopes containing money, lots of money."

"What did he do with them?"

———

"He would give them to Eustace Weller, in the back room by the fire, and then leave. He never stayed, not even for a drink."

"Did Mr. Weller accept the envelopes?"

"Yes. He would leave the money lying on his lap, or on the chair next to him, while he was drinking. He drank quite a bit, usually staring at the fire, sometimes talking with one or t'other of the girls. He talked about his children, in Boston. He had seven children. They lived all in one room, in the North End, he said."

"Did he say the money was his?"

"Oh no. He would say, 'I wish I could keep this, or give it all to you, Katie, or Connie,' or whichever girl, 'but I got to give it to the lawyer.' Then usually he would say, 'But he'll never miss a slice off a cut loaf,' and he would take out one bill and give it to one of the girls, and he would go upstairs. 'Thanks for the drink,' he would say to me, and generally he would wink. He was a gentle fellow, God rest his soul."

"What denomination were the bills which he removed from the envelopes?"

"They were twenty-dollar bills. Bless my heart, every bill he took out was a twenty-dollar bill. Those envelopes were stuffed with them!"

Judge Seabury brought his gavel down on the pulpit five times, attempting to silence the room.

"Not guilty," he said. "You may go, Miss Tiverton. I will see counsel in chambers."

———

———

THE day before we had to pack up for the last time, I felt I had to clear the air with Grandma about what I had seen in Thayer's Wood. After breakfast I offered to help her wash up. This was not a customary chore for me.

"You have something to tell me or ask me, son," she said while drying a dish, without turning around.

"I saw you in the wood on Midsummer's Eve." This was a bluff.

"I know you did, son. I followed you most of the way to the orchard, to make sure you'd be well set up. Your shirt was like a beacon. I thought you'd remember either the apple tree or the oak. I had asked Henry to mention Thayer's Wood to me in church so you could hear."

"You knew I was there?"

"It was better than trying to explain things to you, on a sheet of paper. Don't you think?"

"Yes ma'am."

"Do you understand, Jamieson? Believe me, I have tried to find answers through the church, and at one point in my life felt that I had. Do you understand why Charles Moncrieff had to be disregarded?"

"Because he told us we had to submit to the flooding?"

"Submit to the flooding, submit to his Lord—the one you can worship only in his church, by a great coincidence."

"Did you burn down his church, Grandma?"

"I suspect he burned it down himself, that he had a racket going with the insurance fellow. The insurance company is located in Iowa, they paid right up, probably didn't know

---

the building was about to be bulldozed if it hadn't burned."

"Do you really think he would do that?"

"I can tell you your preacher accepted money from Curley's men, to make sure this thing happened, right from the beginning. He told them it was for the church, of course."

"He was the church, right?"

"Very good, Jamieson. In a way that was his job for the church, to try to have everyone go quietly." She grimaced. "He wanted to denature us, to deny the divinity in us."

"Pretty strong medicine for so early in the morning." Uncle Ed had appeared in the doorway. "You get that from Sir James, or from your pal Nietzsche?"

"It's the right medicine any time of the day, I'll thank you. Why don't you go spend your sixty-dollar cut at the fancy new store in Orange?"

Uncle Ed's eyes narrowed. "You been going through my things?" He stepped into the room.

"Ed, you poor old fool, you've been so transparent these last three months nobody'd have to do more than look at your face to see what you'd been up to. Even Francis knows; he's been observing you. The sheriff has a ledger from Eustace Weller's office, where the dumb sumgun wrote down the amounts paid and to whom. But he's not going to use it: this will all be history in four days."

"This was going to happen anyway, Marion! Sometimes you just have to be practical."

I had never heard Uncle Ed address Grandma by her Christian name before, so I knew the earth had shifted.

"You know you got to get out and don't come back," she said.

"No one's coming back anyway, Marion. You're sick, you're dreaming. In two days this room we're standing in will be bulldozed, and in four days it'll be underwater."

Uncle Ed walked straight to Enfield Centre and got Larry Palow to take him to the train station at Orange in a buckboard. I never saw him again, so I don't know whether he bought himself another new suit at the fancy store. Maybe he found another town where he could be the clerk, maybe he didn't.

Ancestors is one thing, but looking back on it, I don't think Uncle Ed was a real connection to Bill Hardiman. Even if they were flesh and blood.

———

Hannah and I packed our things and left the house early in the morning. The bulldozers were scheduled to come around 10 A.M., and I knew I couldn't watch. We arranged to meet Grandma in Enfield, or what was left of it, at 4 P.M.

We walked into town with fruit in our pockets. There was nowhere to buy lunch, even if we had had money. The only buildings still on Main Street were the post office, the bank, and Lawyer Kincaid's office. We sat on the hill across the way, eating our fruit. There had been quite a lot of demolition the last few days. The crews were no longer careful to tend the fires, as it wouldn't matter if they did burn out of control. The scene reminded me of pictures of the bloodiest battles in France during the Great War, or Shiloh, or Cold Harbor.

———

While I was thus musing, a door slammed and a man marched out of one of the buildings opposite us, clapping his hat onto his head. It was Lawyer Kincaid, doubtless going to his home in Ripton, for the last time, after a hard day's work.

I looked at Hannah and she at me. She spat out a plum pit and nodded.

We waited until Lawyer Kincaid was two hundred yards down Main Street, then began to follow a course parallel to his, keeping to the hilly country to the side of the road. When Kincaid got to the turnoff for his place in Ripton, we slowed down, but he kept right on going, past Darey Pond and the switching yards, to a spot a mile from the beginning of the Wachusett tunnel. We hung well back.

Two men were waiting for Kincaid. They were the men on trial for Hammy's murder. They sat talking on the embankment of the parallel tunnel, the one with no water in it. I whispered to Hannah that we could get to within a few feet of them by creeping through the tunnel, could make out what they were saying through gaps in the roof. In five minutes we were close enough to hear.

"You've got to get out of here," Lawyer Kincaid was saying. "If you don't take the stand you'll hang, and if you do you won't keep your story straight. I've never seen such terrible witnesses. I can't wave my arms and scream about due process. They've got evidence! I can't cause another mistrial. Timmy, you were supposed to burn that lumber, what got into you?"

Timmy was sniffling. "I did burn it," he said, "but I must have dropped a piece. We each had two, six was a lot to carry.

———

I asked Eustace to help me but he said to keep quiet and do my part, told me not to bother him. I'm dead sorry. I didn't mean to hurt anybody, I must have dropped it."

"What do you mean you didn't mean to hurt anybody? You whacked Hammy pretty good. From behind, too."

"Well, you were shaking his hand, in front."

"Shut up, both of you," said Kincaid. "Eustace Weller killed Hammy, and don't you ever forget it."

"Eustace? But Eustace—"

"I said shut up, Timmy. For your own good."

Now the young man began to sob convulsively. Someone clapped him on the back, saying, "There, there." My guess was it was not Lawyer Kincaid.

"It's all because of the money," Timmy managed to get out. "Why did there have to be the money?"

Lawyer Kincaid's voice was firm. "Money is the oxygen of public decisions, son," he said.

"What'll happen if we don't leave?" asked the older man.

There was a pause. Then Lawyer Kincaid, sounding pleased, said, "Maybe I'll have to use this to protect the project and the workers and Mr. Curley."

"What's that?" said Timmy.

"Easy, son," said the older man. "It's a revolver. But you needn't use it, Mr. Lawyer, sir."

"If I was going to, I'd use it on you, Earl," said Kincaid.

At this point I shifted my weight to get a better angle to hear, and dislodged a stone.

"What the hell was that?" Kincaid barked. Timmy and Earl scrambled off the bank into the woods.

Lawyer Kincaid had the opposite reaction. He ran back along the embankment, looking for an opening. He always did what you didn't want him to do. Must have been a great lawyer in court, always pressing.

Fifty yards behind us he found an entry and began barreling through the tunnel. I could hear him panting. I could have negotiated every inch of that tunnel and side shaft blindfolded, so I grabbed Hannah's hand and took off at a dead run. We heard Lawyer Kincaid trip over a loose stone once or twice, swearing a blue streak, but all in all he seemed to be keeping up the pace. After a minute there was a roar and a flash behind us, and a high whine close by my ear.

"Turn into one twenty-one," I puffed. We had to get out of the straightaway, although the condition of the side shaft was uncertain, as there had been cave-ins over the years. We veered left into tunnel 121 just as another round from the revolver screamed past us.

We had to clamber over piles of rock, which cost us precious seconds, but Lawyer Kincaid would have to do the same. I reached for the wall to steady myself and pulled loose a boulder that would have crushed my leg, had it not rolled past me.

I knew that tunnel 121 curved back around into the main shaft in half a mile. Until then it was straight as an arrow, so we remained for the time being in an unlit shooting gallery, where even a ricochet could find us. I was beginning to succumb to terror when there was another blast from the revolver, followed not by an echo but a deeper rumble, which continued to build for half a minute. We made the turn and kept running, but it was clear that matters were out of human hands now. The roof of the main shaft and the hill above it were collapsing. We would either be free as larks or buried alive.

In a moment we saw a crevice of light and squeezed out through the opening. There was some glow left in the sky as we walked back along the top of the tunnel embankment, prepared to jump whenever necessary. Near the end of the main shaft, we heard a yelling and pounding from ten feet beneath us.

"Maybe he'll use his revolver one more time," I said.

"I hope he doesn't," said Hannah. "I hope he's out of ammunition."

We never knew how much air he had, or how long he lasted, because neither Hannah and I nor anybody else ever went back to that part of Ripton. I doubt Lawyer Kincaid died from too little air; more likely too much water, when the flood he had been praying for swept over the tunnel two days later.

I sometimes let my thoughts turn to Lawyer Kincaid at the end. Lawyer Kincaid finally fetching justice, without the process he so prized. Lawyer Kincaid, who said he doubted Hannah's every word, himself a ghost locked underground.

———

THEY held an inquest into Lawyer Kincaid's disappearance on the morning of the flooding. The district attorney said otherwise they would lose jurisdiction. Sheriff Richards was the only witness. He described the facts surrounding the first trial of the two Woodpeckers, including Eustace Weller's

———

drowning. The foreman asked his opinion as to what had happened. There was no objection. The sheriff said the three surviving coconspirators appeared to have fled and that under the circumstances, there was no reasonable expectation of their return. The coroner's jury agreed. Once again, I did not have to testify.

The Quabbin Reservoir

T H E Y let me and Hannah and Caleb stand on the Winsor Dam in Ware to witness the beginning of the flood. Another crowd was up at the Baffle Dam on the side.

Now that the moment had arrived, I was confused and did not know what to look for. I expected phalanxes of walking catfish to appear on the hilltops and descend to the valley bottom, to take up a new home.

Frank Winsor himself threw the handle to close the locks at the dam. Nothing happened for several minutes.

"Maybe it won't work," said Caleb. I felt no emotion so positive as hope, however. My insides had been burnt out.

The east branch of the Swift puddled and became unrecognizable as a river. The plain that formed the west side of Enfield grew soggy, then disappeared.

"We walked that road two days ago," I said to Hannah. She nodded. She must have remembered what happened on that road, but appeared to be thinking of something else.

A half hour later, Hannah turned away from the Valley.

"Where are you going?"

"I'm going for a walk."

"You're not allowed inside the boundary, you could get trapped."

"I'll choose my steps."

I moved toward her.

She put her finger to her lips and with the same finger pointed to the ground, signifying I was to stay put. "I'll see you, again and again," she said. "Soon."

I could have stopped her if I had taken her arm. I could think of nothing but the passing of my physical world. I wanted to be there, to be a part of the occasion. I stood and watched Hannah walk the length of the embankment, then down the hill to the road that led to Prescott. I watched her hips and torso swing the whole way. She looked back at me and I waved. While I was waving there was a snap in the air over my head, startling me. I looked up and saw the huge flagpole, newly installed at the side of the dam, with the flags of the United States, the commonwealth of Massachusetts, and the Water Supply Commission straining in the breeze. Still waving, I looked to the Prescott road, now empty. I thought nothing of it, turned back to watch the waters.

———

———

I stood on Winsor Dam until dark, spent the night in a lean-to the Woodpeckers had constructed near the Baffle Dam, and got up early to resume my vigil. I wanted to see how the Valley would fill up, whether it would offer resistance. There were engineers and clerks hustling about in the morning, but they knew better than to initiate conversation with me. Patches of fog hung in the Valley, and a light rain fell. I was glad of that.

The hills of Enfield lay at my feet. Our farm was not visible, but I could tell it was gone. The big fields, the dusty roads, my swimming holes and hiding places—they were obliterated, gathered, merged under a smooth canopy. I wanted to lift that canopy and peek under, to see the houses and trees as they stood before Curley's men marched into the Valley with weapons more deadly than those carried by General Lincoln.

I was surprised the land received the waters in silence: I had expected an outcry of some sort, at least a rumbling from deep within the earth. Perhaps after the rape that had occurred the land was grateful to be covered over, not to be seen in such a state, barren and ridden with sores.

Grandma brought me pears and plums for lunch. We ate in the meadow below the dam, at freshly painted picnic tables.

"Is Hannah coming over?" I said.

"Haven't seen her today," said Grandma.

"Not even for breakfast?"

"She was gone when I got up, about six. I thought she might be here."

———

"Tell her I'll save a plum for her," I said.

I thought of Hannah saying she would see me "again and again." What did that mean? I returned to my work. Hannah was more important to me than my physical world, but I returned to my work of watching.

When I climbed back to the top of the dam an unfamiliar landmass rose out of the mist directly before me. I was startled: it must have dropped from the heavens, a sign of powerful displeasure. I looked left and right to take my bearings, to calculate where in the Valley this rock castle had fallen. I saw it had tumbled in the area of Mount Lizzie.

A chilly breeze caught me unawares, causing a shiver. As I rubbed my shoulder I looked back at the new peak and recognized it. It was Mount Lizzie, or rather the top of Mount Lizzie. I had never seen the peak without the shoulders.

At that moment, for me, the Swift River Valley ceased to exist. I turned away, climbed down the embankment, and set off along the Prescott road in search of Hannah.

At first I walked slowly, my hands in my pockets. Without knowing why, I withdrew my hands and began to trot. I pictured Hannah waving, saying she would see me "again and again." I began to run.

Under a canopy of maples I saw a figure running toward me. I squinted, trying to make the figure into Hannah, but it was too big. I recognized the coat first. It was Sheriff Richards. He stopped in his tracks when he saw me. I walked up to him as though in a slow-motion dream. I knew and I didn't know. He put his hand on my shoulder and looked me in the eye.

"Hi, Sheriff, how are you?" I heard myself say, fending off the inevitable.

"Oh I'm all right, Jamieson, but I've got some awful bad news for you. One of the spotters on the perimeter in Prescott saw something white in the water at the foot of Mount Pomeroy, where the old Twynham farm used to be, and a rowboat was sent out. I'm sorry to tell you it was Hannah Corkery, Jamieson. I'm afraid we've lost her for good."

I nodded.

"The water wasn't even over her head," said the sheriff.

So she had lain down like Kathleen Connley, lain down on the Twynham farm. She'll have friendly company there.

I never went to see Hannah's body, any more than I returned to the farm after the house was bulldozed. I wanted to deny that she had moved on. I think I was right in this. Her name was not forbidden later, I would use it in discussions with Grandma, but always as though I was referring to a third person, rather than to part of myself. That deadened the pain somewhat.

Even after the waters rushed over her, Hannah's body had not moved. Is that attachment to place, I wondered, or attachment to one's ancestors? It gave me pleasure to recall my argument with Hannah on this point. I was glad we had not reached a conclusion, my plan being to keep up that argument until I join her to resume it in person. It can't be long now.

―――――

AFTER the flooding, a lot of the elderly couldn't adjust. Mary and Dan Winship both died within six months. Grandma said Mary died of a broken heart for the Valley, and Dan of a broken heart for Mary.

―――――

———

FRANCIS the handyman disappeared when we had to move and was never heard from again. The next March, Miss Ettie Clark had twins at the hospital in Worcester, a boy and a girl. No husband appeared, in fact no man. She never married. I felt that her situation put shame on all men. She must have been a great comfort for those children. She was a great teacher.

———

CALEB Durand was killed on Guadalcanal Island, shot in the head by a Japanese sniper. Caleb was my best friend, but in a way I didn't feel so bad about his death as I did about little Sammy Richards. There's something wrenching about an accident. At least someone was trying to shoot Caleb, and he was trying to shoot him.

Caleb's father called me over to their new place in Marlboro and showed me the telegram. I read it to myself. I opened my mouth to say I was sorry but nothing came out and I saw the big man was biting his lip. I left without a word, except to mouth "thanks," and took a rowboat straight to the shoulder of Mount Zion, in the reservoir, where I retrieved our three silver dollars.

———

THE moving was hard on the Mullally family. They settled at first in New Salem. I used to visit Pudge. He said he

———

had nightmares every night. He had to go to a new school, in his bare feet and overalls. The teacher complained his buttons were scratching the furniture. He had to stand on newspapers because of his muddy feet. The kids made fun of Pudge in his new school for being the son of a counterfeiter. When Patrick got out of prison, he moved his family to Brooklyn, New York. I judged that would be the end of any connection between the Mullally family and the commonwealth of Massachusetts, and good riddance.

In this I was mistaken. Patrick continued his life of crime as a fence for stolen jewelry, and Pudge grew up on the wrong side of the law and died young in a shoot-out with police. But Pudge's son became a government prosecutor in New York, moved back to Massachusetts, and was elected United States senator here. He is serving as such at this writing. There were whispers about how he got there, but that was nothing unusual in Massachusetts politics in the 1990s, or the 1930s for that matter. America is a land of endings and beginnings.

P R E A C H E R Moncrieff was promoted by the church and given the charge of a huge establishment and congregation in lower Manhattan. He became a popular figure in the drawing rooms of the East Side. I imagined him raising a subscription to build a railroad, any railroad. He could do it. I wondered whether he ever found what he was missing.

FRANK Winsor, the chief engineer for whom the great dam is named, was called as a witness in a legal case brought by a subcontractor against the commonwealth. The plaintiff's attorney asked him whether he had ever accepted payoffs in connection with the construction of the dam. Winsor replied that he certainly had not. The lawyer showed him a document purporting to be a receipt for monies paid, and asked him if that was his handwriting and his signature. Winsor gagged, grasped his temples with both hands, and fell to the floor of the courtroom, dead as a stone. The dam still stands, however, and his name and likeness figure on a large plaque at the overlook.

———

JIMMY Toolbox took to the hills and died of exposure the next winter. Thus ended his standoff with the law.

———

DAVID and Annie Richards moved to Worcester. He became the elected mayor of the city, as famous in central Massachusetts as Curley was in Boston. He kept a picture of his son, Sammy, on his desk, and showed it to anyone who visited the office. I went there several times. He was always glad to see me. "You know Sammy," he would say by way of introducing the picture. "I do, I do," I would say. "And how is the Heart of Africa?" "Still beating," he would say.

———

———

GRANDMA got a place near Basking Ridge, in the part of Ripton that wasn't flooded. This was right by Doc Crocker's, so he didn't have to come so far to visit. After a while those visits ran into each other. Grandma and Doc Crocker were married at the Town Hall in Belchertown on the first of May, 1939. Grandma chose the date. A justice of the peace said a few words—a very few words, as Grandma cut him off when he was not halfway done.

"That's enough, Robert, get to the point," she said. "We've got to put a stop to all this living in sin that's been going on."

"Yes ma'am," he said. "I now pronounce you man and wife." I was there, I heard him. I was looking for young men painted green and playing pipes to show up, but none did.

Doc Crocker smoked as much as always, and his cough was worse than ever. Grandma was happier than she was before. When Doc got to coughing so bad he started shaking, she would walk up beside him and put her arms around his chest until he settled down. They're both gone now, but they were married and happy for over twenty years. He saw sixty-eight and she saw eighty. "He took me off the shelf," she would say, circling her hand behind his waist. She invited me to be buried in Ripton next to them, and I think I will.

———

———

———

Myself, I went off to war like Captain Shays and like Caleb Durand, except I came back. The war was boring, until the wreck. I was in the merchant marine in the North Atlantic. My dominant memory is the sight of ice in the rigging. I liked to pretend it was ice in trees during hunting season. You couldn't squint and look for horizontals, though: a ship is unnatural and has plenty of horizontal lines.

We never saw a U-boat. One night we were rammed by a troopship carrying G.I.'s to France for the offensive that took the Allies across the Elbe. It was the *Queen Mary* or the *Queen Elizabeth,* I never knew which, converted for the occasion. They were under direct orders not to stop for any reason, since they had two thousand souls on board and could not afford to offer a target to the German submarines. So they kept steaming on. In the engine room, three of our boys were killed instantly, and four of us diced up. I was the luckiest of the four, as I got the use of my left arm back, through physical therapy. Two of my mates had enough flesh blown away so you could see they were skeletons underneath. I saw the skull on one and the rib cage on another. Forty-five men were adrift in small boats for three days. The middle of nowhere on the ocean is different from the middle of nowhere in the woods. The doctors said if the troopship could have stopped for us they could have saved a few of the boys who didn't make it. I need to say, though, they did a good job for us at the vets' hospital in Holyoke, when I got back to Massachusetts. Those people were dedicated.

———

I had never seen salt water before the war, only smelled it that one time, when the hurricane came through the Valley and raised the dead. Now if I never see salt water again, it will be too soon.

———

I shouldn't complain, I've done all right. I didn't marry, though I set up shop with Annie Hulce for a few years. Annie was the girl whose mother made her wear patent leather shoes. Her shyness continued into her twenties and became sexually appealing.

It was an exciting time, after the war. I don't think women have ever been as appealing, before or since.

Annie left me for a medium-looking fellow who took her to Ohio, a medium place. Go figure. It's a big country.

I didn't join a church either. I didn't need to.

I consider that I'm married to Hannah, and I'm a parishioner of the natural world. I talk with Hannah anytime I want, and worship in my cathedral anytime I want.

I've never stopped walking the land, touching the trees, hunting, and stream fishing. I'll still lie down on bushes and stare at the sky all afternoon. There's plenty of redtails, and they still don't get along with crows.

A couple of years after the flooding, the Water Supply Commission began to let people go in through gates to visit the buffer zone for the reservoir, ground that was taken but not flooded. I've tramped every inch of what they call Prescott Peninsula, which stretches all the way from North Prescott to Smith's Village and Mount Ram.

———

The summer after the war I was down to the tip of the peninsula, about where French King Brook used to meet the middle branch of the Swift. I was lying on my back, looking up at blackberry bushes, and became aware that something was out of place. There was something near the top of the bushes that didn't belong there. I got up and went to investigate, thinking it might be part of a bird's nest. I like to examine the weaving of nests. The object appeared to be part of a birch limb.

I had to reach up to pull it out. As I did I heard something fall to the ground through the bush. As soon as I saw the stitching I knew it was my canoe. The Indian was gone, but at the cost of a few bramble scratches I rummaged around at the base of that bush till my hand closed on the dough-faced cowboy. Here was a messenger from my past, a part of me that had survived. His expression had not changed.

I'm the same person I always was. Changes come gradually, and by the time you notice them, they've already happened. Five years ago I was hunting deer in New Salem, near the Heart of Africa. I had gone inside and opened a bottle of Hoppe's gun oil, then set myself up around four o'clock in some rocks near the top of the ridge, with an oak at my back and a three-quarters view of the slope and the bowl beneath me. Shortly before dark I heard a stick snap and eased off the safety, keeping my thumb on it: if you let it click, deer will hear it in the next county. I blinked a bit of snow out of my eye. In that space of time an eight-point buck appeared directly below me, fifty yards away, moving slowly right to left. A perfect shot. I covered his shoulder with the scope.

I decided not to fire, and stood up, breathing hard. The

buck took off with acrobatic speed. I admired every jump. I fired my rifle into the air.

I had never passed on a deer before, let alone a buck. This was a part of me I had not known was there. The seed had been planted not far away, when Caleb and I, fifteen years old, crept single file behind a man with a flintlock.

When I got back from the war I went to the University of Massachusetts on the G.I. Bill, studying history and science. After a couple of years teaching high school, I was fortunate enough to get a job at the state college. They started me out in American history, but I transferred to the biology department. I found it difficult to lecture the kids about local history, which is what they were most interested in. I had a point of view about what happened, and about America, and it was getting in the way of my teaching.

America has both gentle and heartless in it. You can live a wonderful life in the gentle part of America, which is most of it, but if the heartless part notices you, it will come snuff you out, and the place you live.

I'm near the places I loved, even if they're under sixty feet of water. I can still see the hills that border the Valley I grew up in. There's plenty of land for the deer. And because of the reservoir, there's more bird life than ever. Wild turkey are everywhere: they're the official state game bird now. I doubt I would ever have seen or heard a loon if not for the Quabbin Reservoir.

Cataclysm makes things stronger. Think of a sapling bent by snow, or walls that have taken a pounding from the weather, or petrified wood. It's hard to say what's for the best, in the long run.

———

It's been sixty-three years since the flooding. There have been changes in the world outside, though not so many in the towns around the Valley. The so-called popular culture doesn't penetrate here.

I know I won't leave the Valley, any more than the fisher-cat who lives in my woods will quit his den. He's probably the great-grandson of the animal who killed the coyote. They could put me in the same plot as my great-grandfather's if it weren't sixty feet deep.

———

I went back to Prescott on New Year's Day 1948. I had said I would. I had the three 1898 silver dollars. I wanted to show them to Hannah and Caleb, to prove to them that I followed through, that I kept my word. I was sure she at least would be there. I wished she was riding with me in my old green Buick and that we were going together to meet Caleb as we had planned.

As I drove north along Route 202, which they now call Captain Daniel Shays Highway, I turned to look at the reservoir from the high point in Belchertown. I never saw the water, because right there in the passenger seat, fourteen years old with freckles, was Hannah Corkery. She had her hands folded in her lap. She had turned her head to look at me, was smiling at me. She still had the chip off her front tooth. It was good to see her. I felt warm and cool at the same time, I can't explain it.

I was flooded. Everything was fine. It didn't matter it was

———

a raw gray day. I loved raw gray days. It wouldn't matter if I let go of the wheel. The car would either steer straight along Route 202 or it wouldn't. Then I'd get some other experience. But Hannah would be there in the front seat. So in the worst case, the car would plow into a ditch and I would be thrown over onto Hannah's lap. Onto her frock, cream-colored with a pattern of blue windmills.

"I brought the dollars," I said. I shifted my eyes to the road for a second to be safe, then turned back to her, smiling, my heart full. She was gone. I pulled the car over and stopped. She was gone.

"I'm sorry," I said. "We're supposed to meet Caleb," I said.

I drove on without saying anything more and turned in at gate 17. I drove two miles through the woods. I didn't look to my right because I thought she might be there when I stopped the car. I turned off the engine and got out, still without look-ing, and walked around to the passenger door. I opened it and waited a full minute. Finally I allowed myself a look inside the cab of the automobile. There was a burr on the front seat where Hannah had been, but it might have blown in while I was holding the door open. On impulse I got back into the car on the passenger side and sat for several minutes in Hannah's seat, propping the door open with my foot. Snow covered my leg.

I got out of the car and closed the passenger door, taking care not to make a noise. I didn't shake the snow off my leg. I turned southeast and hiked down the spine of the land. When I came to the edge of the reservoir, Mount Pomeroy was in front of me.

The reservoir was frozen solid. Heavy snow was falling and blowing across the surface in gusts. It looked like smoke, curling upward. I sniffed. All I could smell was the cold.

I had on my long johns under a pair of flannels, a red-and-black checked wool parka, and a lined cap with earflaps. I was a match for the weather. I could see the spot at the foot of Mount Pomeroy where Hannah's barn had stood, where we found the silver dollars, where Hannah's body had been found in the water. The wind was in my face. I bent forward, shoved my hands in my pockets so I could pinch my thighs to keep my fingers going, and trudged across the ice. It was slow going on account of the wind. It took twenty minutes to get on top of the old Twynham homestead.

I positioned myself at the spot where Hannah had been found, near as I could tell. The barn had been in a gully. Now the site was thirty feet offshore. Standing on the ice and looking down, I drew the three silver dollars out of my pocket. I was raising them to my face when there was a shriek from above me. I dropped the dollars. I expected to be plucked into the sky. I felt pulsing in my chest and throat.

I staggered a few steps and looked up. A bald eagle was circling my location, half a mile up, screaming. Eagles will do that all day when they have lost a mate. But I hadn't shot an eagle, I reassured myself: I've never shot an eagle, or even a crow.

I turned my back to the wind to get a better view of the bird. Eventually it soared off to the east, disappearing over the ridge of Pottapaug Hill. I remembered the dollars and fell to my knees, but there was snow everywhere. I made several circles, scraped the ice bare with my hands until they bled. None of the coins was to be found.

I stood up, shaking with rage, and glared at the sky. I could see nothing through my tears. I felt the eagle had robbed me of something. I shook my fists.

"Leave us alone for five minutes. All I want is five minutes," I said. I knew it was a lie. I wanted my youth back, I wanted forever.

I felt tired and sat down on the ice. I thought of the eagle. It had marked the spot of Hannah's death. Perhaps of Hannah's birth, too. Hannah, who never had a child's room in a home of her own. I rubbed my eyes, scanned the sky. A pair of eagles was gliding to the south, and now began wheeling over the great dam that had destroyed my world.

"Not a bad marker," I said. Not a bad marker for a girl who was ignored in death as in life.

You ought not to feel bad about nature reasserting herself, I thought, or be troubled by her rhythms. Perhaps it was not the Boston boys who had prevailed in the Valley after all. Come April or May, this ice will melt. Hannah will have our dollars in good time.

And so she has, for the last fifty-three years, as we planned.

———

I read accounts in the local press and even the Boston papers now and then about life in the Swift River Valley towns in the time before the flooding. Yesterday a young

———

woman stopped by my house in Pelham. I live two roads over from Captain Shays's home. Pelham in the old days tried to commit suicide: it had a history of voting to annex itself to other towns. Finally it got cut in half.

The young woman walked up the steps and knocked on the door of my house. She had black hair and wore glasses, had an intelligent expression to her face. She said she was moving west to get away from Boston and was working on a retrospective on the Valley for the *Christian Science Monitor*. I said I didn't mind talking to her. We spent an hour. She asked if anything had seemed missing in the other pieces I had read in the newspapers. I told her they got the farm routines down pretty well but didn't get around to the fact that life in those days was free of care. She told me she knew I was going to say that before I said it. She said she'd never lived in the country but felt as though she already knew me.

"It was not a bad life, you don't have to feel sorry for me," I said.

"I know better than that," she said, staring at me.

"Thank you so much for your time," she said when an hour was up. She had nice manners, seemed older than her years. Her manner was familiar to me. I was surprised she had not grown up in the country.

"What else am I going to do with my time?" I said. I quit teaching eight years ago, but I didn't tell her that.

"Could I possibly stop by tomorrow, teatime? I'll bring some Irish tea, to make it worth your while."

"That'd be fine," I said.

———

I've been feeling tired all day today, but in an hour or so the young woman whose name I don't know is coming by to fix me some tea. I'll tell her more about the Valley. I think she'll understand.

ABOUT THE AUTHOR

William F. Weld is the author of the *Boston Globe* bestseller *Mackerel by Moonlight* and of *Big Ugly*. He was the governor of Massachusetts from 1991 to 1997 and is a former federal prosecutor. He lives in New York.